DOUBLE COVER

ISBN-10: 0991232429
EAN-13: 9780991232420

www.mysterycaper.com

DOUBLE COVER

A WARREN KINGSLEY MYSTERY

SHERBAN YOUNG

COLUMBIA, MARYLAND

Cover art and design by Katerina Vamvasaki.

1 — BAD FOR BUSINESS

"I'd really appreciate it if you'd keep my name out of the paper, Sheriff."

Sheriff Ernest Ballard regarded the other man blankly.

Having spent the past three hours questioning guests of the Berwald Island Inn about the murder of Thomas Redding—a wealthy businessman found bludgeoned to death in his hotel room—the officer had hoped to call it an evening. He had made it as far as the lobby when this chiseled man with a square chin cornered him by the front desk.

At four in the morning a small town sheriff is not at his most hospitable. "Who were you again?"

The chiseled man frowned. "You talked to me five minutes ago."

"Oh yeah? Yeah, of course. You're... Help me out, sir."

"Kingsley. Warren Kingsley."

Ballard considered the name, spoken by its owner with such obvious self-admiration that he almost felt ashamed that he couldn't place it. "Kingsley. Kingsley... Oh yeah. I remember you now. You were the victim's bodyguard."

"Now you got it," said Warren. "Anyway, about the paper. This won't do my reputation any good if the press gets hold of it. Not that it was my fault, you understand."

Ballard stifled a yawn. "I'm not really sure what I can do at this point, sir."

"No?"

"Not really."

The bodyguard took it well. "Well, I know you'll do your best," he declared, and with a manly slap between Ballard's shoulder blades, he disappeared into the night.

The sheriff glowered after him.

Disentangling himself from a rack of Berwald Island Attractions, against which the other's parting gesture had hurled him, he made his way to the front door. About two-thirds of the way across, another obstacle appeared in his path: a much shorter obstacle, small-boned, with thinning hair and glasses. Ballard remembered this one. Eliot Peterson, the dead man's executive assistant.

Since arriving in town earlier that week, the deceased had surrounded himself in a veritable army of wing-tipped muckety-mucks—and there were none more muckety than Eliot Peterson, corporate twerp. Ballard didn't like him.

"Any word on the search for Mr. Luften yet?" asked the assistant, staring up at the sheriff with sharp, analytical eyes.

Ballard shook his head. Frederick Luften had been some sort of advisor to the dead man and allegedly the last person to see him alive. At the moment his whereabouts were unknown.

"Nothing yet."

"A shame. Well, I know you're doing your best, Sheriff."

Ballard was getting a little tired of people saying he was doing his best. He was doing it, but that didn't mean he liked people saying it. Too exhausted to retort, he nodded gruffly and said, "Goodnight, sir."

It was not his night for smooth exits. No sooner had Peterson left than a narrow door in the back of the room opened, and a heavyset woman in a floral muumuu shouted, "Hey there!"

"What?" Ballard asked his sister.

"Did you clear out the corpse yet?" she bellowed. As the inn's owner and manager, she naturally took an interest in these things.

"They carted it away almost an hour ago."

"And about time too! It's bad enough having all these corporate hotshots infesting the place this weekend. Now I have to listen to you and your young imbeciles tramping up and down the stairs! We got guests trying to sleep, you know. Don't think I'm knocking you or nothing, Ernie. I know you're doing your—"

Sheriff Ernie Ballard was no longer present. During his sister's third pause for breath, he had made a swift and effective escape.

2 – No Obligation Necessary

The next morning, the local paper was full of the Redding murder.
Happily for Warren Kingsley, the reporter did not mention his name.

> The murder victim, Thomas Redding, owner of Redding Enterprises and a Boston resident, was murdered under the nose of his notably incompetent bodyguard Walter Kingham, who was staying in the very next room.

Sheriff Ballard sat in his office and read the page while sipping his first cup of coffee of the day. About halfway through the article a heavy hand rapped against the window behind his head, causing him to slosh this coffee across his uniform. He peered up to observe the handsome smiling face of the notably incompetent bodyguard in person.

Warren weaved around to the entrance. "Good morning, Sheriff. A moment of your time, if you would."

Ballard was too busy dabbing French roast from his shirt to issue any greetings of his own. "If this is about the article," he said, "I figured you'd be pleased. My nephew Kenny never has been good with names, and *The Bugle* never checks his facts."

Warren glanced at the folded journal and sniffed. As a matter of fact, mangling his name was far worse than any bad PR, but he didn't mention this. He was far too distraught. "The reporter is your nephew?"

Ballard nodded.

"But you said you couldn't do anything?"

"I couldn't. When it comes to the role of the press, Kenny's got a mind of his own—what there is of it."

Warren shook his head. He hadn't come here to learn about the newspaper industry; nor did he wish to ascertain exactly how much brains the officer's nephew Kenny did have. He had much more pressing issues to discuss than genetics and journalism. "I need police protection, Sheriff."

Ballard's second cup slipped from his grasp and splattered the bottom of his trousers.

"You really shouldn't drink that stuff if it's going to jangle your nerves," the bodyguard observed.

"Did you say police protection?"

"For the duration of the investigation. If you recall, you asked us all to stay in town while you sorted through the case."

"Yes— But— Police protection? *For you?*"

"Police protection, Sheriff. *For me.* Someone tried to kill me last night."

"Someone tried to kill *you*, sir?"

"Someone tried to kill *me*, Sheriff." He turned a plaintive gaze towards a deputy, calling on him for support. "Does he have to repeat everything I say?"

"I'm sorry, sir, but I'm just a little confused," said Ballard. "When did this happen?"

"Soon after you left; around four-thirty. I had just managed to nod off. Suddenly I shook awake and saw a shadowy man looming over me. I felt the barrel of his pistol pressed to my forehead. All he said was: 'Kingsley.' I guess we weren't on a first name basis. Anyway, I let out a yell. At that point, my limbs must have taken on a mind of their own. My leg struck him pretty solidly and he sailed across the room. He ran off after that, though not before I had thrown a pad of Berwald Island Inn stationery at him and one of those Berwald Island Inn pens with the little ducks on them. I really like those pens. I wonder where the inn buys them."

Ballard artfully dodged the subject of duck pens. His shaggy mustache was bristling. "Did you get a good look at the guy?"

"No. But he had a dry, brooding voice, if that helps."

Ballard said oddly enough, it didn't. "Are you sure you didn't embellish any of this, sir?"

"Embellish! I never embellish. How do you mean 'embellish'?"

"I mean could you have imagined or dreamed any of this episode." It was not unusual, he whispered, for the mind to play tricks on you, especially while under stress.

Warren resented the implication. "Episode! It wasn't an episode. It happened. My theory is it was Luften returning to the scene of the crime."

"You think your client's suspected murderer is gunning for you now?"

"That is what I think, Sheriff."

"But if the killer wanted you dead, he had a perfect opportunity to kill you last night."

"Well, I'm telling you he's taking the opportunity to kill me now."

Ballard couldn't figure it. In his experience bodyguards were taken out first, not several hours later when the killer finally got around to it. "Did you even see this Luften last night?"

"No. We've never met, but his name chills me. Frederick Luften. Sounds like the sort of guy who'd poke a gun in your face at four-thirty in the morning."

Sheriff Ballard stroked his mustache. How could he put this? "Kingsley, you're a bodyguard."

"So?"

"So—I would think you would be used to people trying to kill you."

"That doesn't mean I have to like it."

Ballard conceded the point, but as he had told Warren last night, he wasn't sure what he could do. "In case you haven't noticed, I can't exactly spare the manpower."

His eyes fell on his deputy Roger, seated nearby plodding his way through *The Bugle* crossword puzzle. Besides having the resources of a block of wood, the young man had also recently twisted his ankle cleaning out the station rain gutters. It still twinged a little on moist days, Roger would tell you.

Ballard took Warren aside. "Actually, Kingsley, I'm glad you came in. I've been reviewing your record. There are a few things I don't understand. For one thing, I've been having trouble getting in contact with your past clients."

"Oh, you're not going to have any luck there," said the bodyguard, "they're all dead."

The sheriff took a moment to absorb this. "Did you say dead?"

"Of course. People were after them. Never underestimate the ingenuity of the criminal mind, Sheriff."

Ballard would have to remember that one. "Let me ask you something, Kingsley. Are you left-handed?"

"How'd you know?"

"From the angle of the blow, we figure— Excuse me a moment, would you?"

He returned a minute later carrying the murder weapon: an antique golf club. It was one of many old trinkets accumulated by the dead man during his Connecticut journey. It was far from your typical blunt object, dating back fifty years or more, worn and ragged around the handle. It still packed plenty of punch, though.

The sheriff gave it a pensive twiddle as he walked. Of all the odd items that had ever come into the Berwald Island police station connected with a crime, this ancient niblick or mashie or whatever it was still took a distant second to the odd duck now standing at the officer's desk.

Only he wasn't standing at his desk. The odd duck had flown the coop. "Where's Kingsley, Roger?"

"Who, the chiseled guy? He said he was heading back to the inn. Isn't that okay?"

"No, it's not okay! I wasn't done!"

The deputy scooched up in his seat, eyes a-sparkle. "Should we go after him? I got dibs on the riot gear!"

"Just forget it," said Ballard. "Tell you what, though, we're going to keep a watch on that guy. And quit doing my crossword!"

3 – SHIFTING THE PARADIGM

Back at the Berwald Island Inn, Warren was not the only rare bird confined to the nest for the duration of the investigation.

In Kenny Ballard's stirring piece, "Industry Honcho Found Dead in Hotel Room," he had listed over a dozen execs from Redding Enterprises in attendance at the company retreat this weekend. These same execs were now milling about their quaintly decorated bedrooms, pondering what life at the firm would be like now that their boss had been murdered, and wondering why they were being punished for another's good deed.

The Berwald Island Bugle had also run a couple of inches on the hotel staff working at the time of the murder; along with a few paragraphs on the other guests staying at the inn: those poor saps, now unavoidably detained, who had nothing to do with Redding or his Enterprises and were simply there for business or vacation or because they hadn't bothered to consult any reputable travel guides. They, too, had come under suspicion, tarred with the same corporate brush as the milling execs (many of whom had now milled out from their quaintly decorated bedrooms in search of something to eat). In point of fact, the sheriff had no grounds holding anyone here. Other than the elusive Frederick Luften, he had no real suspects and wasn't prepared to make any arrests. But until the ferryboat, run by

Ballard's cousin, finished its "repairs," no one was going anywhere. The guests would just have to suck it up.

At five o'clock that evening, one such guest, a dark-haired woman of a certain exotic and imposing beauty, stood killing her allotted time sucking up a cocktail in the inn's lobby. A foreign born painter (no one knew from where exactly), she specialized in capturing flowers and rocks from an overhead perspective. One critic had described her work as Georgia O'Keeffe meets MapQuest. Cub reporter Kenny, more interested in the artist herself, had described her as Catwoman meets another woman who looks like Catwoman, but others found her aspect a bit too severe. (Warren thought she had scary cheekbones.)

Formidable of cheek or not, her presence made a statement at the Berwald Island Inn. She got noticed.

Across from where she stood her presence was most certainly being noticed by a paunchy man in plaid flannel, lingering in the corner. He was about thirty, flabby, and some would say his head was too small for his body; yet there it was anyway, balanced on top of his thick neck.

He admired the inn's slinky new guest. He loved her slinky black hair, her slinky thin waist and her slinky long legs. He adored her piercing eyes and pointed lips; and he would have been willing to fight any man who thought her regal cheekbones were anything but perfect (although if he had known that it was six-foot-four-inches of Warren Kingsley who offered the opposing viewpoint, he might well have agreed to disagree). Trevor Green thought a lot of Vanessa Skinner, and for once in his humble life he was prepared to do something about it.

But not now. For now, like the artist and her paintings, he would amuse himself by admiring his subject from afar. Their time would come.

He refocused himself on his duties. Although he did not always act like it, he was the inn's new handyman: and he demonstrated this fact now by taking out a lightbulb and screwing it into a sconce. This finely honed handiwork completed, he reached for the light switch and flicked; but not before taking another gander at Vanessa.

If Vanessa had noticed her secret admirer, she was doing a very fine job concealing it. She was currently gazing out at the frigid New England landscape—perhaps considering immortalizing the ice-covered fern at the end of the porch; but in actuality merely wondering when her next drink would arrive. (Ice-covered ferns had their place, she was sure, but at the moment the only ice that meant anything to her was the kind that rattles around inside a martini shaker.)

"I bet you knock 'em dead back home," said a voice behind her.

Vanessa turned and stared. A middle-aged woman, short-haired and long and drooping of frame, had sidled up beside her. She was simpering slightly, as if she knew a juicy secret.

"If you paint half as good as you look, honey, you must really knock 'em dead."

Vanessa Skinner's face softened, or became as soft as her features would allow. Nodding politely, she spoke in an indeterminate European accent, the kind that made the men of Berwald Island melt. "It is nice of you to say this."

"You're the foreign girl, right—Vanessa? The painter?"

"I do the painting," Vanessa agreed.

"Art's a hoot," said the woman, her smile ever-broadening. "Judith Carr," she revealed, extending a bony hand. "I'm the motivational speaker."

"You motivate the speech?"

"I motivate the people," said Judith proudly. "Redding Inc hired me awhile back to light a fire under upper management, get the firm thinking outside the box. That's what we've been doing this weekend."

"There is a fire at this firm?"

"Not for me. I was a little concerned at first, but I spoke to them earlier and they say my services are secure. They're going to need someone to help steady the helm now."

"The hum?"

"Helm."

"Helmet?"

"Helm," Judith insisted. "I'm going to help steady it."

"Ah," said Vanessa, now fully cognizant. "This helmet, it is being studied?"

"I wouldn't know anything about that," answered the motivational speaker. (No one ever said anything about her being a motivational listener.) "That's not my area. This murder is something else, though, isn't it?"

"It is not what it is?"

"Sorry?"

"It is not, as you say, a murder, but something else?"

"Exactly. And you know what that means, don't you?

Vanessa really didn't.

"It means we're all stuck here for the time being. It's a bummer, but what can ya do?"

"Kenya dew?"

Judith Carr nodded, recognizing a perfect cue when she heard it. "I'll tell ya what I'm gonna do, Vanessa. I see this as the perfect time to refocus my efforts at the company. Take the firm in a new direction. Push the envelope."

"The killer, he has sent this envelope?"

"I'm sure you're right," said Judith. "Oh look, here's one of my attendees now."

On the other side of the dimly lit lobby, a few feet before you reach the dimly lit dining room, a lean, ponytailed man in stylish specs had come strolling in from the inn's fitness room. He hadn't gone there to exercise—he just wanted to see what a fitness room in Berwald Island, Connecticut, looked like, and now that he had, he was content. He was wearing his favorite sport coat (blue cashmere), his second favorite sport shirt (pima cotton) and a smile which, when you came right down to it, was rather sporty in itself. He was jaunty. If you had asked young Mr. Blake why he was so chipper, he would have explained that he was enjoying his time away from the office. His life as a junior exec at Redding Inc was stifling and unrewarding. Berwald Island might not have been his first choice for a vacation spot, but now that he was stuck here he couldn't have been happier. He enjoyed the fresh air and the new faces.

At the sight of Judith Carr, yoo-hooing at him from across the lobby, his own face went pale and the fresh air deflated from him in an audible gasp.

"Yoo-hoo," repeated Judith.

She remembered him distinctly from the banquet the previous night, sitting in the first row, all keyed up by the power of her speech on Statistical Analysis of a Positive Workflow.

"I simply love his name, Vanessa. Harvard Blake. Sounds like a college football rivalry, doesn't it? 'Harvard-Blake, all tied up at the half.' Oo-ee, over here, Harvard!"

She shot off after him, and Harvard Blake, not quick enough on his feet, found himself pinned in at the stone fireplace.

It was true, he had been at the banquet last night; and he had taken a chair in the first row. Contrary to Judith's view, however, he had actually been squirming in this chair, deeply regretting the epic fatheadedness which had led him to sit up front.

"There you are, Harvard!" she panted. "I was about to sketch out an exercise on personal and professional boundaries for our next meeting. Everyone will need to bring an egg and three rubber bands. You can help me set up."

"Oh ah," said Blake, backing into the stone hearth.

Nearby, a stuffed moosehead gawped down at him from its post over the mantle. It, too, had once learned the danger of careless wandering.

Vanessa Skinner had grown bored with the plight of Harvard Blake. She cast her heavily made-up eyes around the room: past Harvard and his forced smile; past the main door where Trevor Green was screwing in another lightbulb; past the front desk and the bored-looking innkeeper seated there; and finally past the empty dining room, where she would have no choice but to eat dinner tonight. Her glance fell on the creaking staircase, but this time she did not move past. She had seen something worthy of her attention now.

Warren Kingsley, bodyguard stud, was descending.

4 – Company Roll Call

He came down the steps and circled past Vanessa, Judith, Blake and the sympathetic moosehead. He went to the front desk. The manager, who looked a little like a moose, glared up at him.

"A guy's coming to meet me," he informed her. "A real bruiser. When he arrives, let me know, okay?"

The manager sniffed. Although a married woman and no longer a Ballard by name, she would never lose that slight superciliousness that ran in the family.

"Your associate's already here," she said, pausing to take a languid sip from her cup of cocoa. "He's waiting for you in the lounge."

Warren frowned thoughtfully and headed across the lobby. A moment later, he returned, frowning as thoughtfully as when he had left. "Are there any other lounges?"

The manager shook her head, and for a third time Warren frowned (thoughtfully). He proceeded back across the lobby and into the one and only lounge.

A distinguished man with a round face and a short yet sturdy build stood as he reentered. "Mr. Kingsley, a pleasure. I am Mahrute. The agency sent me."

Warren shook the stranger's hand. The latter had an extremely firm grip, especially for a man with such an unimposing demeanor.

He had short, dark hair and an olive hue to his skin. His mustache, a pencil sketch compared to the forest Sheriff Ernest Ballard had culti-vated on his lip, was thin and well-groomed. He wore a dark gray suit, a dark gray tie and a canary yellow vest: overall a presentation that contrasted with Warren's tan slacks and wrinkled T-shirt. It oc-curred to Warren that Mahrute looked more like a butler than any-thing.

"You're the bodyguard, right?"

"I am indeed."

Warren continued to frown. When he called the security agency this morning and asked for reinforcements he expected them to send him someone a little more orthodox. Not that this pocket-sized vari-ety didn't have its good points, he was sure, but right now he needed muscle, not high tea. "Did they explain the setup?"

"Not exactly. I know you are Warren Kingsley, Mr. Redding's bodyguard, but as Mr. Redding is now deceased, I am a little unclear as to whom I am here to protect."

"You're here to protect me," said Warren.

Mahrute blinked twice but otherwise betrayed no emotion. "You believe you are in danger?"

"That's about the size of it, Mahrute. Mahrute... Is that your first or last name?"

"Last. My first name is Borodin."

"Borodin Mahrute," Warren repeated, not liking either terribly much.

"My family was musical."

Warren blinked twice but otherwise betrayed no interest in this statement.

"My parents named me after the composer Borodin. It's actually a rather funny story. A good friend of the family, who was named after the composer En—"

"Yeah, fabulous," interrupted Warren, nodding. He hadn't asked for the Epic of Borodin. "I guess I'll call you Mahrute, then. Ready to get to work?"

For the next hour, Bodyguards A and B sat silently in the lounge. The evening shuffled by, and eventually the dinner hour arrived. The two men dined in the inn's deserted restaurant.

The manager, also the head server now that the murder had sent most of her staff home with the heebie-jeebies, lumbered out to take their orders. Not a people-person, she did not veil her hostility, giving Warren a particularly piercing glare when he asked if there were any specials on the menu tonight.

Warren wasn't at his most cheerful either. He was beginning to tire of Berwald Island's less than cosmopolitan atmosphere. Prompted for his order, either the cod cake sandwich or the tuna cake sandwich, he ordered the cod cake, but he didn't like it. He didn't know what cod cake was but he knew he would hate it.

He was beginning to hate everything about Berwald Island. He hated the hotel, the shared bathroom, the mocking police department, the sea air, the seafood and the quaint cobblestone streets. He even hated the name. What in the world was a Berwald anyway?

Hoping to soothe his troubled spirit, he slipped a small leather notebook out from his pocket and began to scrawl something. After about a minute of this, he looked up and noticed Mahrute observing him.

"I sometimes like to jot things down," he explained. "Professional observations."

"That's very thorough of you."

"That's me," Warren replied, pocketing his professional observations for the moment. "So where you from, Mahrute?

"I was born near London. As a boy, my family and I traveled extensively throughout Europe."

"Oh yeah?" Even though Warren had traveled often himself, he had never left the country, unless you counted Canada, which Warren didn't. "You must speak a lot of languages?"

"I speak four languages fluently, and can get by, so to speak, in half a dozen more."

"I tried to learn French once," said Warren, fondling the basket of biscuits. "So where do you buy your suits?" he asked.

Before Mahrute could reply, the manager dropped two fishy platters in between them and floated off. Warren followed her departure with a scowl. He angled back around and submitted his sandwich to the same sullen glare.

"Is cod supposed to look like this?"

"I believe so."

"What's this on top?"

"I believe that is paprika."

"You sure it's not arsenic?"

Mahrute said he was sure, and Warren replaced the bread.

"You wouldn't want to trade, would you?"

"No problem," the bodyguard's bodyguard remarked, as they exchanged platters.

"I think she has it in for me," Warren explained. "Not that I want you to be poisoned or anything, Mahrute. But that's why I pay you the big bucks, right?" He bit into the sandwich. He hated tuna. "Anyone ever poison one of your clients?"

"Not that I recall."

"Someone set a black mamba loose in my client's bedroom once."

"Indeed? A somewhat clumsy way to commit murder, I should think."

"That's what I told the coroner. Whoever whacked my last client did it much more efficiently."

"And who was your last client?"

"Andrew Hastings, the Mob informant. He drove his car off a cliff into the ocean. They think someone cut his brake lines. So you're British? Know any spies?"

The conversation continued along these lines. After forty solid minutes of trading stories, most of Mahrute's past remained shrouded in mystery. It seemed pretty clear to Warren, though, that if 007 happened to stop in for the weekend it would probably turn out that Mahrute had once saved him from the clutches of a double agent, and it would only be a matter of time before the two were guzzling brandy and laughing about the good old days.

Over coffee, or a close approximation thereof, Mahrute broached the subject of the Redding murder.

"Had Mr. Redding many enemies?"

Warren snorted his cappuccino (which is to say the odd cream and cocoa concoction the manager was attempting to pass off as that beverage).

"Many? No, not many—only anyone who had ever met him. Some men collect rare antiques, Thomas Redding collected enemies," said Warren, who had heard the line once on an old cop show. "Actually, he collected rare antiques too," he added.

"The sheriff must have his hands full sifting through all the suspects."

"The sheriff has it easy," snorted Warren again, this time taking in a sniffle of cocoa the wrong way. "Who has to sift? All he has to do is lie back in his sheriff, uh— what do you call those things that birds look down from?"

"An aerie?"

"Doesn't sound right. Anyway, all he has to do is lie back in it and scoop up Luften when he strolls by. Easy."

"You believe Frederick Luften to be the only viable suspect?"

"Why not? He was shady, he and Redding had had words previously, and I saw him fleeing the scene."

"I was not aware that. You saw Mr. Luften?"

"It was around eight. Redding didn't want me present at the meeting. Said they had too much personal stuff to discuss. But I happened to be coming down the hall with some ice, and that's when I saw a man in a hat and coat scurry out from Redding's room and make a bolt for the back exit. I thought about following but I was under strict orders not to disturb the negotiations, so I went back to my room and ordered dinner. Mackerel." He shook his head sadly, and not just because of the remembered fish. "If only I had known my client was already dead. But I didn't think. And now I'm going to have to collect my fee from the estate. Do you realize how long these things take to go through probate?"

Mahrute took a sympathetic sip of coffee. "It is odd that Mr. Redding dismissed the services of his bodyguard on the one night he was supposed to meet with such a shady character. I understood from the agency file that it was a certain belligerence on the part of Frederick Luften that prompted your client to hire you in the first place?"

"It was, but I guess the old coot figured Luften wouldn't try anything with me in the next room. Whatever they were talking about must have gotten heated, and fast."

"You were not privy to the reason for Mr. Luften's visit?"

Warren sniffed in the negative, as if to say no one told him anything.

Mahrute continued, "I suppose it is always possible that Luften is innocent in this affair. Anyone who knew of his meeting with Mr. Redding might have killed the latter in order to frame the former, the former having already established himself as a menace to the latter. I merely toss this out as a theory."

Theories were fine by Warren, assuming he could keep track of all the formers and latters. He seemed to have counted about forty-six of them.

"And, as you have already stated, there are plenty of suspects," said Mahrute.

"No doubt about that," Warren agreed. "In fact, there's one sitting behind you right now. German chick. Looking seductively in my direction."

Mahrute was well-aware of the young lady seated some twelve feet behind him. The angular beauty calling herself Vanessa Skinner. Although he understood her to be from Prague.

"She's definitely a suspect," Warren went on. "She's been flirting with me the whole trip. I mean, real come-hither stuff."

"You consider that a motive?"

"No. But I'm starting to think she was trying to get to Redding through me. And she creeps me out. Oh, and her reason for coming here—painting pictures of rocks? Preposterous! Don't they have rocks in Bulgaria?"

"I believe they are known for it."

"There you go, then. And from what I hear she wasn't at the banquet the night of the murder. I mean, she probably wasn't invited, having no connection to the firm, but that doesn't change the fact that she has no alibi. I heard her tell one of the deputies that she was in her room watching television at the time, but that still would have given her ample opportunity to slip out, possibly during a commercial break, sneak into Redding's room, and come hither to the back of his skull."

"An interesting theory."

"You're not the only one who can come up with them. Oh, and then there's Harvard."

"Mr. Redding's alma mater?"

Warren frowned. If Mahrute was going to switch to one of his twenty-six different languages he might consider ringing a bell or something to let him know. "Never mind Redding's mother. I'm talking about Harvard Blake, the guy sitting by the window, looking squiggly-eyed into his coffee cup."

He drew Mahrute's attention to their fellow guest: currently peering into the depths of his mug. It seemed the company's youngest ponytailed middle manager had discovered some alien object within his beverage and was trying to decide whether to send in a rescue team or simply let it swim to dry land on its own.

Mahrute had already met Mr. Blake. In fact, while Warren was in the restroom and Mahrute was waiting to be seated, he and Blake had shared a pleasant word about the sea air. Blake had said he found it crisp and bracing, while Mahrute thought it bracing but not all that crisp.

"Is Mr. Blake also on your list of suspects?"

"I don't have a list," said Warren peevishly. "It's all up here." He tapped his forehead. "He's a nice enough guy, Blake, but he had motive. The boss man was holding him back. According to him, every time he tried to climb a little higher on the industry ladder, there was old man Redding with his steel-tipped boots, ready to kick."

"And what is this industry exactly?"

"No idea," said Warren, who also didn't care. "The only reason Redding hired him, Blake thinks, is his name. Redding went to Harvard Business School. But he never would have advanced beyond lower management at the firm. Not while Redding was calling the shots."

"How is Mr. Blake's alibi?"

"It's okay, as alibis go, but it has holes in it. Blake left the banquet early. He skipped out on his responsibilities and went for a walk, before heading back to his room."

"How do you know this?"

"I met him on my walk. We passed each other in the hall about eight-thirty, plenty of time for him to go take the old man out while I was away."

"I'm curious," said Mahrute. "Did no one at the banquet think it strange that their employer was absent?"

"Oh, Redding had no intention of attending. He had 'people' for that sort of thing. People like Harvard Blake. Curiously enough, Blake had nothing bad to say about the boss when we ran into each other. But he was very caustic about Judith Carr. I don't think you've met her. She's the so-called motivational speaker."

"Would she have any reason to do Mr. Redding harm?"

"Besides the norm, I suppose not. Actually, yes! When Blake was talking about her, he said Redding couldn't stand the woman and all her motivational muck. He probably would have canned her after the retreat was over, but now her job is secure. She couldn't have killed him herself, though—I hear she was at the banquet all night—but she might have hired someone. Someone like Luften."

Mahrute considered this tidbit with another careful nod. "You seem to have made a very complete study of the inhabitants."

Warren shrugged and said it passed the time. "I mean, I don't know everybody's story. The tubby guy standing over there, for instance. The handyman. Someone said he was only hired a couple of weeks ago, but I don't know where he came from. Nor do I know why he is trying to screw that lightbulb into the hanging ficus."

The moment Warren said this, the handyman Trevor seemed to realize his mistake and shifted the bulb over to the right.

Still staring at Vanessa, he was now attempting to screw it into a portrait of a cartoon duck dressed in rainwear.

"That's pretty much everyone. Except Peterson, of course. But Peterson couldn't have done it."

The name was unfamiliar to Mahrute. "Peterson?"

"Eliot Peterson, the wonder twerp. He's this annoying little guy who worked for Redding; sort of his right-hand man."

"I have not met Mr. Peterson."

"You didn't miss much. He was with Redding before I came on. Did everything for him. Ran his affairs, balanced his finances. Everything. Sometimes I got the feeling that Peterson was the one behind the entire company."

"Sounds dynamic."

"If you say so. Now that Redding's dead, he will probably be let go. I doubt he'd be simpatico with anyone else at the company. He and Redding were made for each other. Pound for pound, you will never see another employer-employee crosstalk act more in harmony."

"It doesn't sound as though he would gain anything by killing Mr. Redding."

"No. And besides, he has an ironclad alibi."

"What alibi is this?"

"Me," said Harvard Blake, joining them at the table.

5 – MARGIN CALL

H e had only intended to pass by with an airy wave. But hearing them discussing the murder and knowing he had the inside track on the Peterson alibi, he lingered, awaiting invitations.

Warren's "Oh, it's you, Harvey," seemed as good an opening as any. He took a seat and shook Mahrute's hand, formally introducing himself to the man with whom he had shared those stirring views on the sea air.

"Did I hear you mention the P-man? Little Lord Peterson?"

Warren's "Yeah Harvey, you did," urged the junior exec onward. "Odd being a guy's alibi. You feel as though he should thank you somehow. Not that I went to any special effort or anything. Just told the truth."

"You are the one who confirmed Mr. Peterson's whereabouts?" asked Mahrute.

"Confirmed the crap out of them. In fact, until I made my break for it he and I were virtually inseparable."

"Why—" began Warren.

"Did we stick together? The guy glommed onto me, that's why. It started around half past six, in Mr. Redding's room." Blake took a bite of one of Warren's pralines and threw his mind back. "I was in conference with his corporate majesty when the hobbit Peterson came in and said a Mr. Luften was here, itching to see him. The king didn't seem all too pleased. He muttered something under his breath and dismissed me and the midget Peterson with an agitated flourish. He was good at agitated flourishes. It was almost time for the banquet anyway, so Peterson and I made the long trek across the hotel, all the way to the detached cabin suite our innkeeper whimsically calls a business center. For the rest of the night, Peterson never left my side—which, on top of Judith Carr's motivational speaking, was no picnic, let me tell you. When I finally made my escape he was seated with a trio of yuck-a-pucks from marketing, and from what I gather, remained in plain sight of them until well after midnight. His whereabouts are sealed in titanium."

"Is it possible that he could have left the banquet for a couple of minutes," wondered Mahrute. "Long enough to dispatch Redding?"

"I'm telling you he didn't leave it long enough to pee. We took care of that together too," Blake grimaced. "Another thing I could have done without. I don't know about you, but I can never go with someone talking fiscal responsibility at me in the next urinal. That was before dinner was served. After the doohickeys arrived."

Mahrute confessed to a certain ignorance when it came to corporate lingo. "Doohickeys?"

"Antiques. They were delivered during Judith's speech. She was just telling us all about shifting the paradigm and pushing the envelope when these antique delivery guys came in and interrupted her. I will always be grateful to them."

"Antiques," mused Warren. "Oh, that must have been the old codger's statue."

Blake said it was the codger's very thing. "Apparently Redding had gone on one of his patented shopping sprees the day before and was having everything delivered to the hotel. There was some mixup, though, and they brought the junk to the banquet instead of Redding's room. Peterson seemed pretty put out by it. He told them to leave the statue in the parking lot, while someone—well, me, in fact—made a very amusing comment about the old lunatic having a marble likeness of himself commissioned. The delivery guy said it was actually a likeness of Napoleon, which I consider splitting hairs. There was also a small oriental rug and a couple of other knick-knacks which I helped Peterson stick away in one of the spare storage rooms down the hall. I guess he carried it all back to Redding's room himself after the banquet."

On the table in front of them, the flame of the dinner candle shimmered violently. Warren Kingsley had said "Ha!"

"Carried it himself, my elbow!" said Warren. "If you want a tale of woe and antiquities, I've got the tale for you." He took a gulp of cold coffee. "It was around twelve last night and I had just managed to drift off to sleep, when who should call me, but Eliot Damn Peterson. He told me he was having trouble bringing in a statue for Mr. Redding. I was still pretty groggy and tried to explain that I wasn't a lawyer, whereupon he said a *statue* not *statute*, and I said *oh, a statue, why a statue*, and he said something about his head throbbing. Well, anyway, we got it worked out in the end, and I got dressed and went to the parking lot at the other end of the hotel, and there was Peterson standing next to a marble goofus in military attire."

"Napoleon," said Blake.

"Whatever. He said he couldn't find a dolly and would I mind lugging it while he went back for the lighter items; and I said sure, that's what they hired me for, lugging statues; and he said good, glad to hear it, and I grabbed the statue. It wasn't light. I suppose it shouldn't have surprised me. Redding was always asking me to tote his crap all over the place. I sometimes felt like he wanted a mover more than a personal security expert—a personal security expert, I might add, who once worked on the staff of an elite European count. That is, until somebody killed the elite European count with a jar of pickled onions. I think Redding enjoyed seeing me lifting for his amusement. I was nothing more than some modern gladiator in a hernia belt to him. I told Peterson I was seriously considering filing a complaint against his boss with the agency, misuse of personnel, but with Redding dead, I guess that would seem weird now."

Mahrute agreed that satisfaction for a job well done is frequently better than dwelling on any particular grievance; while Blake, no stranger to office politics, added that satisfaction was the important thing, all right.

"How do you kill a man with a jar of pickled onions?" he wondered.

Warren explained that it involved hurling the item down from a twelfth story window, and Blake nodded and said that would do it. "So it was you and Peterson who brought the junk back to Redding's room? I thought I heard you banging about the corridors."

"Peterson had Redding's rug, and I had Redding's statue, but when we got to the room there was no Redding. Peterson thought it odd that the boss wasn't in his bed, and after a quick search of the grounds we came back and found his bludgeoned corpse under the coffee table. It's always the last place you look. It had been there the whole time, you see, but it was slightly out of view, obscured by all his antiques and crap."

"Then the cops arrived, banging on doors and waking everyone up?"

"About twenty minutes later," said Warren. He liked to get these things right. "They figured Redding had been dead for at least four hours."

If you asked Harvard Blake, he had been dead at least forty years. He would have shared this witticism, but at this point Judith Carr arrived in the dining room to arrange and organize some nourishment, and Blake ducked out behind a businessman from New Brunswick.

A few minutes after that, the innkeeper shuffled in and informed Warren that he had a call at the desk. The bodyguard excused himself and headed for the lobby.

On the way, he noticed Mahrute following him. "What are you doing?"

"Tracking your activities."

"Really? I never follow my clients about."

"No?"

"No. I give them their space."

"I see. I can wait over there, if you prefer?"

Warren nodded meaningfully and picked up the receiver. Waiting for Mahrute to situate himself in a leather chair several paces off, he turned and said "Hiya" into the phone.

A mellifluous female voice answered on the other end. "Is this Warren Kingsley?"

"The one and only. Who's this?"

"I'd prefer to remain anonymous. I have some information for you on Frederick Luften."

"Luften? What about him?"

"I'd prefer to tell you in person."

"Super. Do you like cod?"

The voice on the other end seemed unable to reply for a moment. "Meet me in the market downtown in half-an-hour," it said. The line went dead.

Warren replaced the receiver. "Does Berwald Island have a downtown?" he asked Mahrute.

Across from where they stood Trevor Green crouched behind a love-seat, slightly out of view like a bludgeoned corpse. He was screwing a lightbulb into a tiny nightlight in the wall, and listening intently.

6 – BEAR MARKET

Forty minutes later, Warren and Mahrute took a cab to the specified location and learned that Berwald Island, Connecticut, did, in fact, have a downtown. On drizzly Sunday evenings, it amounted to more of a ghost town of unoccupied gift shops and seafood restaurants struggling for business. With thunderstorms brewing outside of New Hampshire, and the rest of last season's snow still melting into the harbor, a definite nip had crept into the air that night. Warren bundled up and rubbed his hands. He would have worn a hat but hats always made his head look bulbous.

"I don't think she's going to show, Mahrute."

Mahrute stood alertly by his client's side. "Perhaps we should have phoned the sheriff."

Warren curled a lip at the statement, much the way he had curled it back at the inn when the other had first made the suggestion. "I have already explained that. If Ballard came, the girl would surely spot him, get nervous and scoot. Already she may have gotten spooked seeing you here."

"Even still, the sheriff has men at his disposal. They could fan out and conceal themselves."

"You haven't met these deputies, have you?"

Mahrute admitted that he had not, and Warren gave another of his gentle head waggles. He was well-versed in the Berwald Island police.

"You're too accustomed to excellence, Mahrute. These are bumpkins, total bumpkins. Told to fan out, they would trip over their own feet. Asked to conceal, they would stick out like a forest fire. My guess is Ballard's mustache alone is visible from space."

"I'm sure you are right. I still feel—"

"Try not to let emotions enter into it," Warren recommended. "Icy nerves, that's what they call me."

Their discussion now concluded, Warren stepped over to the town bulletin board and stood scrutinizing an item of significance pinned there. Reaching up, he slipped the paper inside his pocket and without further comment turned his icy gaze back to the empty market.

"My fingers are cold."

Mahrute handed over his gloves. (Back at the inn Warren had insisted that he did not need any. Hot hands, he had said they called him then.)

"I believe this may be the young lady now, sir."

A curvy woman in her late thirties approached. She had light brown hair, a bright and wholesome face, and an air of silent strength which Warren found immediately appealing.

"Which one of you is Kingsley?" she asked, reaching them.

Warren frowned. "I am, of course."

"I told you to come alone."

"No, you didn't."

"Oh." She tightened the sash of her raincoat and moistened her lips, the latter of which Icy Nerves thought looked soft and kissable. "Well, I meant to tell you that. Not important. Listen," she said, "I saw the newspaper today."

Warren frowned again. He had only skimmed the article, but he knew he had not come off well. "Yeah, about that— Kenny had it in for me."

"I'm talking about the part where they mentioned Luften."

"You know something about him?"

"I know— Hey, what's your banker's problem?" She nodded toward Mahrute, who had slowly detached himself from the proceedings and was scanning the darkened street.

He met Warren's stare. "I would like you both to step behind that dumpster."

"What are you talking about?" asked the woman. "What sort of banker are you?"

Warren concurred. "What's up, Mahrute? You look ootsy."

Mahrute did not answer. His well-trained eyes had focused on an approaching sedan; a brown sedan, with its headlights off. It increased its speed. Before Warren could speak, the sedan slowed. The window rolled down and a pistol barrel stuck out. Suddenly the quiet cobble streets filled with gunfire.

Mahrute had already yanked Warren and the woman into the alley and covered them both with his body—quite a feat considering that Warren alone was twice Mahrute's size. An instant later, the car was gone.

Warren stood and flicked a portion of Berwald Island from his person. "Of all the nerve!" he said.

He was astounded. First they came at you in your bed, then they tried to poison you with questionable cod, and then when none of that worked, they shot you. Some resort town this was! He looked around. Something seemed amiss.

"Hey, where's the girl?" Twirling on his axis, he made out a whoosh of tan overcoat moving up Caribou Drive in the opposite direction.

The girl was on the run.

Warren Kingsley did not hesitate. The fact that the sedan was long gone did not affect his decision to climb out from behind the dumpster and give chase. He was a member of the brotherhood of the Massachusetts Institute of Security Specialists, and MISS did not let opportunity slip its grasp. This woman—this lovely, gentle woman with the kissable lips—knew something about Frederick Luften, and Warren was determined to find out what.

It was all about professionalism.

He galloped up Caribou, crossed Elk and took a sharp right onto Wapiti. He hurdled ice patches. He ducked tree limbs. And when some variety of bubblegum wrapper sailed up and became entangled in his hair, he batted it away with a manly disregard for his coif that became him well.

Speed and impressive physical prowess do not always equal success, however. Warren was only now realizing this.

The alley he had clomped into was a dead end.   The brown haired blur he had observed vanishing into the shadows there was actually a Maine coon cat known to its owners as Lily.   He was no good at giving chase.

Slowly backing away from the feline with a wary tread—Warren did not care for cats—he was about to head back the way he came when from out of the shadows—not the same shadows, different shadows—a figure sprang out and lunged at him with a knife.

Warren was growing weary of Berwald Island CT. First they try to poison you, then they try to shoot you, then they— Well, he didn't like it.

Having sprung backwards and toppled over a pile of trash, he jumped up again, kicking lobster traps from his path with the same disdain he had shown the gum wrapper. The figure, dressed entirely in black with matching black ski mask, came at him with the knife, the blade gleaming in the light of a nearby streetlamp. Warren was ready this time. He curveted out of the way and swung a mighty fist at the ski mask. It missed and the mighty fist hit a metal drainpipe.

"Oo, oo! Cold fingers," he yipped, and the knife came at him again.

This time he caught the assassin by the wrist and held it there long enough for the ski mask to butt him in the face. Staggering back, he saw a boot, and this boot met his jaw.

He crumpled to the ground. The figure jutted toward him once more, only to be repelled by the arrival of Mahrute. And about time too, thought Warren.

There was nothing theatrical about Mahrute's technique. He did not spar or play it coy. When the assailant attempted to engage him in hand-to-hand combat, the bodyguard's bodyguard calmly and efficiently beat the person down in a series of well-timed chops. As quickly as it had started, the brawl was over.

He helped Warren to his feet, remembering first to secure the combatant with a pair of disposable hand and feet restraints he always had in his pocket.

"What the hell is going on, Mahrute?" asked Warren.

"It is difficult to say."

"I'll say it's difficult to say. That— Hey, he's getting away!"

Warren was correct. The assassin had sliced the shackles with another concealed knife and disappeared back down the alley. For the second time that evening, their audience had run out on them.

Mahrute apologized for the oversight.

"Don't worry about it," said Warren. "I think you scared him straight. You— Hey, what's wrong with your suit?"

Mahrute glanced down at the hole in his left shoulder sleeve.

"Only a flesh wound," he replied.

Warren was amazed. Taking one for your client. How novel.

7 – STOCK RISES

A small town doesn't see many gunshot wounds, of the flesh variety or otherwise. Nevertheless, the local doc patched up Mahrute's with relatively little difficulty: a considerably smoother process than with Warren, who made a minor fuss about his wrist (injured when Mahrute pulled him to his feet back in the alley) and insisted on pain killers.

Sheriff Ballard arrived as the doctor was finishing up in Mahrute's room. Warren, always glad to help out, provided the officer with muddled and confused testimony, indicating that the car, a four-door or perhaps a coupe, was brown or possibly black if not dark green, and that he was pretty sure that the license plate had letters in it.

The woman he could be more specific about. He noticed that she had wonderfully curved hips, a luscious full mouth and—and on this he could be quite definite—a bold smoldering in her eyes—though he was a bit foggy on her height, weight and hair color. According to Warren, these were not the truly significant details. As he very astutely pointed out, everyone has height, weight and hair color.

Fortunately for Ballard, Mahrute filled in the gaping blanks Warren had left, and the sheriff returned to the station to ponder the investigation.

An hour later, Warren was still reviewing the essentials himself.

"You don't meet girls like that everyday," he said, standing at the window of the hotel fitness room.

Despite his flesh wound, Mahrute didn't want to miss his nightly exercise routine—a somewhat alien concept to Warren, who rarely had to exercise himself. Naturally strong but utterly lacking in any stamina, he was good for short bursts, like chasing women through alleyways, or looking buff in a T-shirt. It was all about the little things with Warren.

"I don't mind telling you, she moved me. She— Hey, stop moving me, Mahrute."

His bodyguard, dressed in a nylon running suit, gently inched his client out of view of the parking lot window (and any passing brownish-black sedans).

Warren took a seat on the rowing machine. Eliot Peterson, the only other occupant in the weight room, walked over and jerked his towel out from under Warren's left buttocks—which was also very buff. "What a woman," Warren sighed. "Honest, real. Funny how it took a man like Luften to bring us together. I wonder what she knows about him."

Mahrute was wondering this himself. He was also wondering when Mr. Peterson was going to turn over the bench press machine. He stood by patiently while the smaller man ran through his regimen. Eventually completing his set of reps, the assistant adjusted his eyeglasses back to status quo, straightened his loose-fitting sweat togs and stalked out of the room. Mahrute waited until he had left before wiping down the bench. It was all about civility with Borodin.

He paused a moment over the weight pin. He frowned thoughtfully, and then moved it up into a more suitable position.

"You feel it was Frederick Luften in the sedan?" he asked absently.

"The sheriff sure does," said Warren. He's putting out an all points whatchamacallit."

"And the figure in the alley?"

"A mugger?"

Mahrute did not object verbally, but his brow definitely took issue with this explanation.

Warren was still musing. "You know, there's something about that alleyway brawler I can't put my finger on. It was after he had knocked me on my ass and while you were beating the stuffing out of him. Something missing. Oh well, it will come to me, or it won't."

The sound of approaching footsteps interrupted his meditations.

"Check that out, would you, Mahrute? And if it's our secret assassin from the alleyway, chop him one in the brainpan for me."

It was only Harvard Blake, coming to pay a visit, so Mahrute left his brainpan alone.

"Hey guys! Heard about the shootout. You bodyguards really know how to get your all out of a resort town."

"Just a trifle," said Mahrute.

"Trifle! The last I heard, Redding's killer had run amuck with an Uzi and filled one of you full of hot lead." He paused. "Neither of you looks full of hot lead."

"Mahrute was hit," Warren remarked with a casual gesture.

"And the Uzi?"

"No Uzi," said Mahrute.

Blake was glad. Getting riddled full of Uzi pellets was no fun. "There was a shootout, though, correct?"

"And a knife fight," said Warren, now lost in reflection on their mystery woman and those oh-so kissable lips.

"You would seem to know a lot about our escapade tonight?" Mahrute asked Blake.

"Huh? Oh, I'm only repeating what I heard from the handyman. He knew all about it."

"Did he, indeed? That is odd."

"Very," said Blake, but he wasn't sure why. He just liked agreeing with Mahrute.

"Did you and the handyman discuss this?"

"Not exactly. I was hiding behind a curtain in the lobby and he was talking to somebody, I couldn't make out who. Or is that whom?"

"Whom," said Warren, now definitely detached.

"You see, I had spotted Judith Carr coming and— well, it's not important. I missed some of the early part of the handyman's conversation. Who knew that bundled burlap disguised sound so well. Did you say knife fight?"

With the bodyguard-dreamer otherwise engaged, Mahrute took up the narrative. In a few well-chosen words, he brought their new acquaintance up to speed.

"Sounds like you had a ball, all right," said Blake. "And you have no idea who these guys were?"

"Not at the moment."

"Remarkable. First Luften, then this mystery figure in a black ski mask."

"I don't think I mentioned the color."

"You said ski mask. I didn't think it was something in a muted pinstripe." He hesitated, considering the tone of Mahrute's remark. "Hey, you don't think I could have anything to do with this, do you? I realize you have to suspect everybody, but come on! Shootouts and judo fights? I wouldn't even know where to buy a ski mask. Guys?"

Mahrute remained round-faced and stoic. Warren remained square-jawed and focused. He had taken out his notebook again and was scrawling something with a lowered head. Neither answered.

For approximately two minutes all that could be heard was the sound of Mahrute's weights clanging up and down on the chain, the gonging of the town clock and, a few feet away, the careful scribbling of Warren Kingsley's pen.

"Anywaaaay," spoke up Blake then, "unless that gonging deceives me, it's two a.m. Sleepy time for the B-meister."

"There," said Warren, shaking out his sore wrist. "Oh hey, Harvey, you still here?"

Blake agreed that he was. But not for long. "Hence the sleepy time for B-meister reference."

Warren said he didn't know anything about this B-meister person. He was pretty sure he had been told the name was Harvey.

"Harvard actually. B-meister is simply my colorful—"

"Did I hear someone say it was two o'clock?"

"I did."

"Anyone about?"

"About what?"

"Around. About. Is there anyone around and about, Harvey?"

"The handyman was earlier, but he's sure to have gone to bed by now."

"With the B-meister?"

"Forget the B-meister."

If only he could, thought Warren. "And Judy?" Warren didn't care much for Ms. Carr, or anyone else who tried to motivate him.

For what he had in mind tonight, her presence was definitely not required.

"Judy headed back to her room," answered Blake. "I made sure of that."

"Perfect," said Warren. "Now we're getting somewhere." He pocketed his pen and pad and swept from the room. Mahrute and the B-meister followed at a puzzled distance.

"This agency of yours," asked Blake, as he and Mahrute made their way down the dim corridor and into a room of dark and pointy objects, "you guys have to take psychological profiles there, right?"

"We do. Why do you ask?"

"Nothing," said Blake, whapping his toe. "I remember studying something in school, multiple personality disorder, and thought perhaps Warren— the eccentric behavior— It's not important," he whispered, ramming an elbow.

The moonlight from the skylight overhead wasn't strong but it was vivid enough to show a faint smile from the bodyguard's bodyguard. "I can assure you that Mr. Kingsley is quite sane." The sound of Warren throttling a coatrack into submission came to their ears. "He's been under a lot of stress," Mahrute explained.

Blake had picked up on that. "Doesn't matter. Now that I think about it, I failed that class anyway."

Mahrute led the way around the remains of the coatrack. "This was at university?"

Blake said it was.

"Not Harvard University?"

Blake said it wasn't. "Yale," he replied.

By now Warren had found the wall switch, and light flooded the room. They were in the inn's kitchen.

Warren took out his leather notebook and extracted a folded sheet of paper. He slapped this down on the countertop, revealing the page to be a glamour photo of a plate of clams casino. Mahrute recognized it as the one the trailblazer had pocketed from the town bulletin board this evening.

Warren clarified, "It's an ad for one of the seasonal restaurants reopening next month. I saw it earlier and knew I had to have it."

"The restaurant?" asked Blake. He had no idea that bodyguards made that kind of loot.

"The clams. If we're going to be stuck here, I want something more palatable to eat. My stomach can't take any more cod. I want clams casino."

Mahrute seemed to feel this was a fair desire. Blake nodded in turn. If the guy wanted clams, the guy wanted clams.

"Well," said Warren.

"Well?" asked Mahrute.

"Well, well, well," said Harvard Blake, just to keep the conversation flowing.

"Wanna get started?" Warren asked.

Mahrute did not follow. "Are you under the impression that I can cook, Mr. Kingsley?" He might have looked like a personal manservant, but once you got past the tailored suit and respectful demeanor, there was nothing more than a savvy, multilingual warrior, who wouldn't have known a ceviche from an egg whisk.

"But you're so worldly, Mahrute, so very worldly. You mean to tell me you're not?"

"I have eaten in some very fine restaurants in my travels."

"There you go."

"Eaten, Mr. Kingsley, not cooked."

"Well, I'm sure between the three of us, we can work this out."

He opened the refrigerator and stared within. He wondered where the chef kept his casino.

"I do not think this is feasible, Mr. Kingsley."

Mr. Kingsley scowled. "You're such a moody little fireplug. Why not feasible?"

"For one thing, there appear to be no clams."

Warren pulled his head out of the fridge. He glared. "I can see that, Mahrute. Obviously we'll have to make them."

"Only God can make a clam," said Borodin Mahrute.

"Not make. I didn't mean make. Improvise. We need something clammy."

Mahrute struggled for a more definitive way of explaining that he did not cook, and Warren frowned. "You're not going to help?"

Mahrute struggled for a more definitive way of saying no, no he was not, and Warren sighed.

"I guess I'll have to do it myself, then," he said.

Other than Thomas Redding strolling into the room, an antique golf club protruding from his skull, almost nothing could have struck Blake and Mahrute as more surreal than the next sixty minutes watching Warren Kingsley prep his wholesome meal. When you've come to know a man as a simple-minded wall of muscle, only good for deflecting the occasional sniper's bullet—and even that not very well—you don't expect to find that he is secretly the Wolfgang Puck of the personal security game and, among other things, knows how to cube a potato with an expert flair. For the first half-an-hour, they sat by silently, watching these developments unfold with bulging eyes.

Warren appreciated this silence. He needed to concentrate: come into harmony with the cream and the herbs, and more or less "be" the quarter cup of shallot, diced. Aside from a twenty second diversion, wherein he asked for some clams and Blake explained that they had been over this and there were no clams, he hardly spoke until the lid was on the pot and the dial turned down to simmer.

"I guess I picked up more from my client than I thought."

"Client?" wondered Blake.

"The client before Hastings. The celebrity chef, Jack Wiggington. He was sort of the Bobby Flay of Vancouver, but less Irish and with more enemies."

"You were his bodyguard?" Mahrute asked.

"For six months." He shook his head. Poor celebrity chef. "Anyway, before someone k— Before I left his employment, he taught me everything he knew; well, most everything. He said he was sick of me standing there looking like a dolt; and if they were going to spend the network's money they might as well get something for it. He used to give me odd jobs to do, slicing and dicing. Eventually, he let me prepare a whole meal. I was actually wrangling with some very troublesome risotto when someone loosened the bolts on a stage light over his head and, um, cancelled his series. Ever since then I've kept all the recipes I developed under his tutelage in that little notebook." He pointed to the leather journal. "I also throw in the occasional tasting note, or idea for improving a dish. I don't know what anything is called, I just go by instinct and memory."

Blake couldn't help chuckling. A culinary savant—what a hoot, as Judith Carr would say. He was overcome. Not since Betty Alderich from accounting flashed her womanly assets one Redding company picnic, had he known of a person possessing such hidden depths. "And when do we get to taste this recipe?" he asked.

"Presently," said Warren. "Perfection takes time."

At ten minutes of three their patience was rewarded. Warren set two steaming bowls of chowder before his companions, and the pair dug in.

"This is awesome," the junior exec gasped.

"Excellent," agreed Mahrute. The evening had been a shocker for him as well.

"What's this in here?" Blake wondered. "I mean, besides the potato and all?"

"The seafood? It's cod. It's all she had."

"Cod!" said Blake reverently. "Cod is awesome! This soup is awesome."

Warren thanked him. "The secret's in the stock," he explained.

"Stock is awesome!" chanted Blake. "I love stock, and I don't mean the Dow! You know," he remarked, sipping, "I could market this soup, and I don't mean the S & P. I've always wanted a project I could sink my teeth into, no pun intended, and this is it. With your skill and my knowledge of human nature, we could make Warren Kingsley the Chowder King of Berwald Island. Pun intended."

The Chowder King simpered gratefully.

He would have gone on to reveal a few more of his secrets, including the dicing of the potatoes and the right balance of salt and garlic, but he didn't have a chance to finish the thought. An unseen hand had appeared from the darkened corridor behind him and bashed him over the head with a long narrow object.

The inn's manager followed the bashing. She always had been an impressive woman with a dust broom. Seeing what she was up against, not burglars but a trio of guests, she sheathed her weapon and stood there, what-the-hell-ing at them.

Blake took up their defense. He explained, with all the charm at his disposal, that they had come down for a quick nosh and it was no big deal, really. His charm did nothing to placate their hostess. If anything, the word nosh seemed to inflame her passions even more.

"Nosh? You think you can come in here at three a.m. and nosh? Is this nosh headquarters? I don't know if you know it but people have been murdered under this roof this weekend, smashed to bits with golf putters, and you break into my kitchen and nosh?"

Warren finally found speech. He had recovered from the swatting and could now give tongue.

"Excuse me, but the door was unlocked. There was no breaking. By the way, I broke your coatrack."

The innkeeper shimmied from the bottom of her worn slippers to the ends of her tattered bathrobe. "I should call the police!" she said. "I should call Ernie and have him cart the three of you off to jail. See how you like your nosh there!"

"Perhaps you would care to sample Mr. Kingsley's fine offering," Mahrute asked her.

She had intended to dismiss the offer with a haughty flourish, but one look at the bodyguard's gentle eyes and she accepted the bowl with a reluctant grunt. No one could rebuff Mahrute when he was looking so kindly.

She sampled. "This is awesome. What is this?"

"The proper way to prepare cod," said Warren.

Their hostess finished the soup in a gulp. "I have to serve this soup! You gotta give me the recipe."

"And what good would that do you?"

She whirled around on him. Her fingers twitched and for an instant it looked as if she might reach for the dust broom again. But she held off. "He's right," she said, almost in soliloquy. "I can't cook. My cook can't cook. You gotta cook for me, fella."

"That would be a no."

"Then instruct my chef. You can do that, can't you? Instruct?"

"Don't let her badger you," Blake piped up. In his capacity as freelance marketer, he had become the culinary bodyguard's staunch ally. "She's not your employer. Your employer's lying bludgeoned in the morgue. I doubt she even has a board of directors."

Warren had no intention of letting her badger him. He hadn't cared for the innkeeper's snotty service at dinner that evening; nor had he appreciated the way she had sneered at him the morning of their arrival when he had asked for a room with a view of the Berwald trees. He saw no reason to help her chef now.

The innkeeper snorted. She had one ace up her bathrobe. "If you don't help me, then you can't use my kitchen anymore."

"Better listen to her," said Harvard Blake, switching gears as the bodyguard's advocate. He had just realized that his bowl was empty.

8 – CUSTOMER SURVEY

Two days later, the Berwald Island Inn premiered what even the sharpest critic would have described as a spectacular array of soups. The bisque was impeccable, the minestrone a work of art, and the cod chowder ambrosia. And this from a restaurant that had never really excelled at the afternoon meal. Like your average Hollywood agent it more or less "did lunch," but it did it furtively and without joy. Lunch had never been the inn's forte. Breakfast was fine. When it came to frying up an egg the Berwald held its own. But lunch and dinner had always left something lacking.

No more. In two days, the inn's total mealtime business had increased by a factor of ten. Famished townsfolk, weary of their own cupboards, started arriving in droves to see what all the hubbub was about. Tables had been brought up from the basement. Servers were phoned and told to get off their dead asses and come to work. They had customers.

And they had Warren Kingsley to thank for it. Once he had gotten started, the culinary juices had just kept flowing. Fancy homemade crackers and garlic croutons had begun flying out of the oven like golf balls off a driving range. And unlike golf balls, they were really good to eat. He had added a handful of salads. He had insisted on fresh baked bread for the sandwiches. He had reorganized the kitchen from the tile up—so much so that when the manager's husband (and fellow innkeeper) Chester arrived home the following morning, having spent the week in New Hampshire, his first thought was that he had gone to the wrong hotel.

"Deirdre, this is excellent tomato bisque," he said, seated at the kitchen table, taking in the various alterations.

Deirdre, though she did not often see eye to eye with her husband, had to agree. The tomato bisque, she said, was damn good.

"It makes a nice change," he slurped. "Food you can eat. I should get stuck in New Hampshire more often."

Deirdre said like hell he should. "Do you know who's been sweating themselves to the bone this weekend, Chester? Do you know who's been working night and day while you were off galavanting around New England?"

"Sure," answered her husband promptly. "You told me his name when I came in. Winston Knightly or something."

"I'm not referring to Warren Kingsley. I mean me!"

"Oh right." Chester was just about to say that. "Of course I knew it was you."

"We're supposed to run this place together!"

"And most days we do. But I have to see my sister sometime. We would have had her here, but you can't stand her."

Deirdre didn't know what this had to do with anything. The point was she had put in some pretty strenuous management this weekend without any help: printing menus, greeting customers, watching Warren teach their chef how to pit an avocado. It wasn't easy. And on top of that they had had the murder. "Everything has been go, go, go."

Chester might have pointed out that a murder could hardly have been all that go, go, go, involving as it does a lifeless corpse, but it never did any good pointing things out to Deirdre anyway.

"Speaking of murder," he said, "I'm concerned about—" He watched the waitresses bustling around them. Chester liked to see his employees working, but at the moment he was finding their presence hindering. "—well, you know," he concluded.

Deirdre, who didn't, asked one of the passing waitresses for another bowl of today's special.

While Chester talked and Deirdre ate, the figure of a man, pale and flabby and wearing way too much flannel for such an unseasonably warm day, moved slowly up the garden path outside the kitchen. He didn't exactly tiptoe—that would have only looked more suspicious and probably a little unseemly—but he did progress at a cautious stride, and that wasn't easy either. Having recently emerged from the toolshed, he was carrying a hefty metal ladder, the sort that clanks and rattles with each step and makes a silent approach almost impossible.

Trevor Green had plenty of reasons why he might be lugging ladders about. He was the inn's handyman, and handymen use ladders. Despite this fine rationale, however, he skulked. He skulked up the rest of the path, across a brick terrace, and was still skulking like an out of shape jungle cat as he hove up along side the inn.

Huffing slightly, for he was not used to this much physical labor so soon after lunch (a delicious bouillabaisse), he slid the ladder into place and got into position. It didn't take him long. After a quick scuffle with a fern, and a short brawl involving a couple of wind chimes— during which the fern got into the thick of it and had to be restrained—he reached the top rung, and could hear a man's voice drifting out through the balcony window.

"I don't see what was wrong with my other clothes," said Warren, standing in his bedroom in his T-shirt and boxers. He was talking to Mahrute and Harvard Blake: Mahrute reviewing some notes on the Redding murder; Blake holding out a pair of pressed trousers, a humble offering to the Monarch of Minestrone.

As decided two evenings ago he had now slipped comfortably into his role as Warren's business advisor, a role that Warren didn't remember authorizing.

Authorized or not, Harvard Blake was there for the duration. Already he had helped get the word out on the soup. It goes to show that anyone can have hidden depths. A man might look like a shallow corporate hotshot. He might have a ponytail and a Bluetooth headset; but deep down in his soul he may not be a total waste. He might actually know how to market the crap out of a soup-making bodyguard, and that can't be all bad.

"Look, I went to a lot of trouble finding these garments. It's not like there's a haberdasher on every corner on this island. I had to sniff out the quality. You'll like these slacks—as Mahrute would say, they're the bee's knees."

"I would not say that," argued Mahrute.

Blake went on, leaning even harder on the slack motif. "They're designer label, Warren, made in Milan."

"And my regular pants were made in Argentina; the Milan of the south. Why change them?"

Blake stepped closer. He placed his hand on Warren's well-formed shoulder until a look from the other prompted him to remove it. "Warren, you're your own celebrity chef now."

Warren didn't want to be his own celebrity chef. Celebrity chefs had to be charming and colorful, and when people grew weary of them, they brained them with loose stage lights. What sort of life was that?

Blake stepped even closer. He placed a hand on the other arm and this time held it steady. "Warren, I'm your head of marketing. You trust me in that capacity, don't you?"

"No."

"Already I've made the inn the talk of the soup-eating town. This is a complex advertising campaign, with you at its core. You're a hit. This is what you wanted, isn't it?"

"No."

"Eventually the people will want to see you. Meet you. The man. The chef. The culinary superman with the refinement of Julia Child and the brawn of Spartacus. You wouldn't want to disappoint your public by looking shabby, now would you?"

"Yes."

"Exactly," agreed Harvard Blake. He was glad to get that all settled. "Now take these slacks and I'll be removing the pins from your new shirt. You'll like it. It's pima cotton."

Warren didn't know what pima was exactly but he knew he would hate it.

Outside the balcony the handyman Trevor stood perched on the ladder, soaking this all in. Although riveted to discover whether Warren liked the shirt, and curious how it coordinated with the slacks, he had other matters to occupy his mind. Most notably, there was another conversation coming through the skylight on his right. The tail end of this conversation drew him in closer.

"Anyway, Deirdre, that's why I'm concerned. I think we should do something."

Trevor peered over the side and saw the woman Deirdre lift her wobbly features and stare; not enough to notice the face peeping in on them from the skylight, but enough to take in the speaker sitting on her right, an averagely built man with wispy brown hair, a small goatee and fishy gaze. Trevor's employers at the inn.

She took a bite of leek from her soup and spoke. "Wha oo me?"

Her husband didn't get it. He couldn't speak leek. He stared at her confoundedly as she swallowed and rephrased, "What do you mean? I don't even know what we are talking about."

"We're talking about my concern. The concern I just described."

Deirdre wasn't following. "You're not still stewing about that prank last week, are you?"

"Prank?"

"The toilet paper around the chimney. I told you it's just kids, those darn Jenkins kids. They're always doing things like that. Kids having fun."

Chester sighed. He always sighed when his wife missed the point. "I'm not talking about the chimney, I'm talking about Ernie."

"Ernie my brother?"

Chester nodded. Her brother Ernie. "I talked with him when I came into town."

"How did you get into town anyway? You never told me. I thought the police weren't letting anyone in or off the island?"

"They aren't, but Ernie allowed the boat to bring me over unofficially, and it was to thank him that I stopped in at the sheriff's office. That's when I saw that he seemed upset."

"The Jenkins kids haven't teepeed him, have they?"

"Of course not. He's the sheriff."

Deirdre didn't see what being sheriff had to do with anything. Kids around here would teepee anything if it stayed still long enough.

"I think we're getting off the track here," said Chester. He was experiencing one of his migraines, curiously absent during his visit to

New Hampshire. "Ernie says he can't detain people here unofficially much longer, and he's no closer to solving this murder."

"He always was a slow one," said Deirdre. "Even when we were young."

"Ernie thinks this mystery man Luften may have accomplices, someone who's helping him hide from the police. Maybe even someone in this very hotel."

Deirdre remarked that Ernie always was prone to overcomplicate things. Even when they were young.

"I'm worried, Deirdre."

"Why? Do you think Luften's gonna murder us in our beds or something? Why would he? We don't know anything."

His wife's reasoning was sound, especially the part about not knowing anything, but Chester persisted. "I'm worried because if Ernie doesn't make any progress, the state police will come in. Ernie said as much when we talked."

"Why? Because he can't solve one murder? He's never solved anything before, why start now? And why should the state care? It's not like Ernie's thrown a shoe or something."

"Thrown a shoe?"

"As in a horse. Thrown a shoe, so they have to shoot him."

Chester pondered this. It was news to him that this is what you did with horses. "Are you sure you aren't thinking of breaking a leg?" he asked.

Deirdre glared. "Why should I be thinking of breaking my leg? Why should I break my leg?"

"Not you. Horses. I think you're thinking of shooting a horse because it broke its leg. Shoot a horse for throwing a shoe and I think people would talk."

This went on for a while, and above them Trevor had to stand there and listen to it. Adjusting his weight on the ladder, he took out one of his prop lightbulbs and played with it in the sunlight.

Chester shifted tactics. "If the real cops show up, honey, they will search—" Another waitress scooted past, and he hushed up. "I think that's a reason to be concerned, don't you?"

Deirdre was coming to appreciate her husband's point. She just didn't like it. "Well, what do you want us to do about it? Solve the crime for Ernie ourselves?"

Chester said not solve exactly, no. Just help.

"I think for starters we need to consider our staff. I'm sure Ernie questioned them, but how well did he probe their backgrounds? Half of them were hired in the last month, and we don't know a thing about them. That new handyman, for instance. I don't know if you've noticed, but I'm sure I've seen him spying on the guests. He— Did you hear a noise?"

Fortunately for Trevor, who had chosen this instant to slip and topple off the ladder, Deirdre didn't hear it. Nor did she hear him scattering the wind chimes, a tin bucket, and a cat, all on his way to the earth. The cat—Lily—was the most vocal.

Chester continued, "What was I saying? Oh yeah. Trevor, the handyman. He's got kind of a shifty look, don't you think?"

Presently the proprietor of that shifty look, now also donning a few twigs and a couple of miscellaneous scratches (courtesy of Lily), returned to his spot at the skylight. Brushing his ears free of leaves and branches, he was glad to hear the conversation moving on. He hadn't caught the segue, being otherwise engaged, but apparently they were now on the subject of the maid Sheila, who Chester thought had kind of a sneering look.

"I'm not saying we can do this alone. I bumped into that English gentleman this morning, what's-his-name—Mahrute—and he said he had some experience in this area and agreed to look into things for us, discreetly."

"That's good."

"I thought so. Nice fellow. Who is he, by the way?"

"He's a bodyguard. I met him in the kitchen a couple of nights ago while Warren was making one of his chowders."

Chester didn't get it. He knew the new soups were good, but getting them their own personal security detail? It hardly seemed necessary.

"They came with Redding. Well, Warren did. He was Redding's bodyguard. That's his regular job, when he's not making soup. Mahrute came along later, as Warren's bodyguard."

Chester understood. Actually he didn't, but he had a rough idea. He should have known that his wife never would have commissioned these men herself. Normally Berwald Island wasn't any place for rent-a-goons. Sure, there was that time old Nick Foster was asked to guard the statue of Colonel Berwald at the courthouse for the night. But that was only because those pranksters, the Jenkins kids, had painted the statue of the colonel in the town square blue the previous Halloween, and while one blue Berwald was okay, two would have simply seemed ridiculous.

"He is very keen to help, and I think he'll get results. If he does, he will save us the trouble of explaining about— Well, you know."

Up above Trevor didn't know, and he didn't care. He was all a-twitter. Mahrute poking around the inn didn't work for him at all.

Perhaps Mahrute would stick with the guests. Yes, surely the guests would be the ticket. Trevor turned back to the left side of his eavesdropping, Warren's bedroom.

"And that is why I think we should focus our efforts on the hotel staff," Mahrute was saying, and out on the ladder Trevor quivered. "In my experience, the root of intrigue at a house frequently begins with the hired help."

"Whatever," said Warren, admiring his reflection in the mirror. He wasn't listening. The pima Harvard had given him wasn't bad, after all. He didn't know if he would feel the same about the imported leather loafers, but he was keeping an open mind. "Hey, speaking of root, did anyone remember to add ginger to the kitchen order?"

Blake, handing him a hand-knit sweater vest, replied that he had remembered it, yes, but the supplier was out. Warren said, "Crap. I want to make something with lemongrass!"

Outside Trevor creaked on the ladder, becoming more a-twitter with each passing moment. They were investigating the staff. Perhaps they would confine themselves to the regular employees. Yes, the regulars. People like the maid Sheila, who even Trevor thought was highly suspicious in her folding and vacuuming. He jerked back around to the skylight, his head spinning.

"And I told him to start with this Trevor character," Chester said to his wife. "He's the most suspicious of the bunch. What do we know about him? Nothing. I mean, he pops up one day and starts handymanning. Who does that? I told Mahrute to talk to Harold about him."

"Harold?"

"Harold Foster, Nick's brother. The guy Trevor took over for."

A thump, followed by the hiss of a cat who has had about all it's going to take for one afternoon, sounded from outside.

"Didn't anyone hear that?" asked Chester peevishly. Ignored as usual, he rotated back in his seat and returned to his tomato bisque.

9 – Modest Earnings

"Explain to me what we're doing here again?" asked Warren, as he, Harvard Blake and Mahrute navigated the rickety back steps belonging to Harold and Nick Foster, townsfolk.

The Foster headquarters lay at the end of the docks on the southern side of Berwald Island: a small, dilapidated property with an antique shop on the bottom level, and a small apartment above that, which the two brothers shared. It was to the second story apartment that the freelance investigators now headed, ascending a wooden deck that seemed to creak and sway with each gentle breeze. The shimmy was especially vivid to Warren, who never liked wind gusts (or anything else that mucked up his hair), and liked great heights even less.

They finally arrived at the top step, a good twenty feet above an unrelenting concrete. Warren reached out and prodded his bodyguard in the ribs. He rephrased his question:

"Why are we here, Mahrute? I could be back at the inn perfecting my roux."

Mahrute answered without turning. "I'm sure I need not remind you of our agency's primary stated purpose?"

"You do if you want me to remember it."

" 'Limit harm,' Mr. Kingsley. I believe if we can assist the sheriff in his investigations, we can avoid any more mishaps along the lines of the shooting two nights ago. We can limit or prevent harm, and I think it is our duty to do so."

"We'll be leaving in a couple days anyway."

"And what of the murder? You have no need to see justice done?"

"Nothing to me," said Warren, who got paid either way.

Mahrute took a deep, soothing breath. "As I mentioned to you back at the inn, it was not necessary for you to come. Either one of you," he added, looking at Blake.

Warren was incredulous. "You expect me to stick around at the inn while the loony Luften is on the loose? Not to mention the hotel chef. I am certain he has a grudge against me. I caught him sharpening his knife this morning. He told me he needed it for breakfast, but all he was preparing was cereal. No, I think I'll stay with you guys, even if you are allowing this investigation to overshadow your regular duties. We're bodyguards, Mahrute, not private investigators. Bodyguards, with no room in our schedules for frivolity. By the way, remind me I need to pick up some ginger while we're in town." And with these stirring words, he led the rest of the expedition across the threshold.

Inside was much like the outside of the Foster home: old and dilapidated, with antiques scattered everywhere. Of all the relics in the room, none were older or more withered than the antique dealer Nick Foster. They had already met him outside his shop.

"There you are at last," he grumbled. "If you want my brother, he is there."

Warren, Mahrute and Blake gathered around the man lounging on the sofa next to the TV.

Both Fosters were gray-haired and bearded with a small potbelly, narrow shoulders and blue eyes; but the handyman Harold differed from his sibling in the shape of his nose (Harold's was more bulbous), the bandage around his right knee, and the fact that his name was Harold. He greeted them with a nod, another keen difference to Nick. Nick had only grunted.

Mahrute began their inquiries. "We must apologize for disturbing you, sir. We can see you are still recuperating from an injury."

"Yeh."

"But we were wondering if you might be able to assist us. Perhaps you heard about the murder at the inn?"

"Yeh."

"We were hoping you could tell us a little about the young man who took over for you in your handyman duties. This is a young gentleman by the name of Trevor Green. I understand that he was available to fill in for you after your accident. More or less on the spot?"

"Yeh."

"This was curious, was it not?"

"Neh."

"We— Did you say Neh?" asked Mahrute.

"Yeh?"

The inquisitor frowned. He was drawn aside by Blake, who had seen this sort of sales resistance before. This required a delicate PR touch. "Do you mind?"

Mahrute stepped aside, watching as Blake leaned in and whispered something in Harold Foster's ear. The handyman's eyes lit with a strange horror and he let out a cry of anguish. It made a change from Yeh.

Mahrute was astonished. "What did you say to him?"

"I said we knew he was hiding something about his accomplice Trevor Green and if he didn't pipe up he'd have the baddest ass bodyguard in Connecticut to answer to about it."

"My word," said Mahrute. He had expected to glean a modicum of information from the ex-handyman, but nothing as telling as this guilty shudder would seem to indicate.

"You have to know how to phrase these things," Blake explained. "The PR touch."

"That and you leaned on his bum knee," said Warren, pointing. Evidently the PR touch involved pressing a hundred and sixty pounds of oblivious marketing guru to an old man's sore joint.

Mahrute made profuse apologies, first to Harold and then to Nick, the latter of whom had stepped out from the back room to see what all the hollering was about.

"We seem to be having trouble making ourselves understood," said Mahrute.

"And why not," Nick Foster retorted. "We're French Canadian. Hal never learned English."

"He's French?" whispered Warren.

"Indeed," whispered Mahrute back.

"Fantastic. Mind if I have a turn?"

Once again, Mahrute moved aside. He was always willing to defer to a fellow multilinguist.

Warren shifted closer, mindful of Blake's pressure point. He took a deep breath.

"WHERE... DO... YOU... FIND... CAMEMBERT...?" he asked, speaking carefully and loudly. "IS... THERE... ANY... CAMEMBERT... IN TOWN?" he wondered.

He stepped back.

"You're right. He's not talking."

Mahrute took it from here. He spoke smoothly and effectively to the prone man, asking him to please excuse his accent.

Harold didn't seem to mind. With a grateful sigh that made his potbelly shake like a Berwald Island porch, the injured handyman finally opened up. The tattered sofa became his stage, the TV screen his golden-hued spotlight.

"*Oui*," he said in reply to Mahrute's questions about the accident.

"*Oui, oui*," he remarked in reply to questions about Trevor.

"*Non*," he answered when the reply wasn't *Oui* or *Oui, oui*.

At the conclusion, Mahrute nodded his appreciation. He translated:

"He was injured in the business center, one of the smaller rooms the innkeeper Deirdre wants to convert into a computer lounge and Wifi hub. I tried to explain what a Wifi hub was but couldn't make him understand. In any event, he was working with the nail gun, he says, when one of his ankles got tangled up in the air cord. The other foot slipped, and the gun hit the floor. It would have proceeded to fill him full of nails, he explains, if it weren't for the quick thinking of the man Trevor. The young fellow appeared as if out of nowhere, scooped it up and turned it off—only misfiring it three times, two of these hitting Harold in the leg."

Warren scoffed. The only time he had ever worked an electric nail gun he had kept the misfires to one, and it had only grazed the person standing next to him.

"He considers himself very lucky," Mahrute continued. "The way the gun was firing nails here and there, it could have easily meant curtains for him, and not the kind Deirdre wants him to hang in the dining room."

The other two amateur investigators absorbed this. Blake asked if he had really used the expression curtains. "And he really has no idea where this Trevor sprang up from? The guy was merely strolling by, looking to save hapless strangers from runaway power tools?"

"Evidently."

"And once rescued," added Warren, warming to their criticism, "he was at liberty to fill in as handyman at a moment's notice? No training necessary?" This was the major point of contention for Warren, who, in order to qualify for their agency, had been required to complete several courses, two over a week long.

"It is indeed a mystery," Mahrute confessed, strolling over to the window. "Mr. Green appears to have been in the right place at the right time."

"I never liked him from the start," said Warren. "Someone should camp out at the inn and watch his every move. If he's here as Luften's man on the inside—"

"There is no need to restrict ourselves to the inn," Mahrute pointed out. "His movements have scope outside the hotel."

Blake and Warren joined him at the window. They watched as a bright plaid flannel shirt passed by the house, attached to the billowy figure of Trevor Green.

"My God!" said Warren. "The dough ball followed us here!"

"I wonder if he's meeting someone," said Blake.

"We shall soon find out," Mahrute replied, moving to the door.

"You go now?" asked Nick Foster. He had reappeared from the back room, this time holding the guts of a 19th century cuckoo clock.

"With many thanks," said Harvard Blake.

Nick Foster gazed back at him. "I know you, I think, yeh?"

"Hard to say—did you see that YouTube clip last spring on the future of the textile industry, with special guest from Redding Enterprises?"

The only phrase Nick Foster understood was Hard to say. "You attended the corporate banquet the other night? My men and I delivered things to Mr. Peterson? The statue and the rug?"

"Oh right, the company banquet," said Blake, frowning to remember. It seemed an age since he was involved in such uninteresting, non-soup activities. "Small island."

"We forgot this," grunted Nick, shoving an ornate military sword into Blake's hands. "It is meant to go with the statue of Napoleon."

"Thanks," said Harvard Blake. But not many thanks.

10 – PUB RELATIONS

Truth be told, Trevor Green had not followed Blake and the bodyguards into town that afternoon; nor had he known that the weather-worn shack he had just passed belonged to his predecessor at the inn. None of this mattered to Trevor. True, hearing Harold Foster's name through the skylight that morning had unmanned him momentarily, but his angst had passed almost as quickly as he now trod the cobblestone streets on his way into town. Looking at it calmly and rationally, he realized that the man Harold didn't know a thing about him, and therefore could reveal nothing if questioned by one, two or forty-six bodyguards all acting on behalf of the Berwald Island police. His cover was safe.

As for the bodyguards themselves, Trevor might have begun the day motivated to track their every movement; but after a couple tosses off a ladder, his enthusiasm for bodyguard watching had been dulled practically to a blunt end, and he was pursing other avenues now.

The avenue he had in mind at the present was much nicer to look at anyway. He could see her in a window as he crested the hill: a striking brunette, best described as exotic, with a cool and indifferent look on her face, best described as pouty.

Vanessa Skinner's absence from the inn, away from her paints (and the bar), might seem strange to those familiar with the demanding schedule of a professional landscape artist. It was that time of day, after all, when a painter ought to have been bustling about with brush and canvas, trying to capture the noonday sun. But she wasn't. She was in Berwald Island's only answer to European cuisine, the Czech Around Café, picking at a grilled watercress omelet. This can be readily explained: she had an appointment (although Trevor would have preferred to think of it as a date).

Up until this point she had been studying the horizon with a steely glint. The perfect artist's survey. In the midst of this survey Trevor popped up at the window, and it was as if the art gallery of her mind had been overrun by the local flophouse.

The way he gazed in at her reminded her of a hapless scarecrow her Uncle Gustav had once run into in his pickup truck during a shortcut through the wheat fields. That same frozen stare, as it pressed its face to the windshield, unable to move.

The living scarecrow pulled himself away and came inside. It was a shame he hadn't arrived a couple minutes earlier, for the sun had peeked out from the clouds to rest on her alabaster face, making her look particularly statuesque. Of course, he had admired her plenty back at the inn (usually when she was standing in profile and hadn't seen him coming). But today was an especially good day for her brand of beauty. The sun only accentuated it.

There was no sun at the moment. Only a gray Berwald Island haze, Vanessa, Trevor and a plate of some kind of room temperature dumplings.

Trevor made a beeline for the table.

"Sorry I'm late," he apologized, taking a seat across from her and running a hand over his closely cropped hair. "Got in a scuffle with a cat."

"It is of no consequence," said Vanessa, nibbling. She took a sip of wine.

"I knew you'd understand. We— Hey, you're eating."

"Only starting," she replied in a dour tone, lightly soaked in accent. Trevor still wasn't sure what accent.

"Oh right. Sure. Right." He motioned to a scruffy-looking waiter standing at the window. Actually it was the proprietor Bruno, but this was an easy enough mistake to make.

Not unlike Vanessa, the restauranteur had been staring out the window. His beady eyes had focused in on one of Harvard Blake's many advertisements for the Berwald Island Inn posted to a telephone pole. He was glaring at this and mumbling something in a grating undertone about soup.

Trevor smiled at Vanessa. "It's great how you found a place in town that caters to your kind of food. Who would have thunk it?" He turned to Bruno. "Um, sir... Waiter... Maitre... Yeah, you. I'll have what she's having. I don't know how to say it in your language. *Orro*—" He looked to Vanessa. "I'm still boning up on my Czech."

"He is not from Czech Republic," she said.

"No?"

"He is from the Cincinnati."

"Ah," said Trevor, thanking her for the heads-up. He concluded his order in perfect Ohioan English. "I just figured, the dumplings— The Czech Café— Doesn't matter. I've been boning up on my Czech for you not him."

"I am not from Czech Republic either," she replied.

This depleted Trevor's enthusiasm somewhat. It had been easier with Harold Foster. They hadn't understood each other either, but at least they had known what language they weren't understanding each other in. "Oh. Well, that's— I thought you said— It's no big deal. You're foreign, that's all that matters."

"What is this you say?"

"Nothing. I didn't mean—" He paused manfully, collecting himself. "Have you thought about my offer, Vanessa? You know, to come away with me once this is all over?"

"I have not thought about this, Trevor, no."

"That's okay. I sprang it on you that day. And then the next day and the following evening. It was just a random thought." He paused again, marshaling his thoughts. Suddenly these thoughts came gushing out of him in a wave of suppressed giddiness. "Vanessa, I am not a romantic man—"

"You were doing the skinning of a cat?" she interrupted.

Trevor stumbled. His giddiness stubbed its toe. "Wha—? Skinning a cat? I—? Oh, the cat. No, not skinning, only scuffling. I got in a fight with this cat, but it was no big deal."

"You were unpleasant to this cat?"

"Not at all. Let's just say it was one of those unfortunate misunderstandings. But we worked it out. I agreed not to land on her from any more great heights and she agreed not to try and scratch out my jugular. We parted on good terms. Vanessa, I am not a romantic man—"

"I thought it was strange that you should be skinning a cat."

"Love does not come easy to me—"

"In Czech they call the cat *kocka*."

"That is why I am not a romantic man—"

"I do speak the Czech."

"—I am not what you would call a—"

"But I am not Czech, as I say."

Trevor, totally put off his stride now, could only stare. "Vanessa?"

"Yes, Trevor."

"I am a VERY romantic man."

"Ah yes?"

"Yes. Really I am. I know we hardly know each other, but I know that we are—that you are— well, I'll say it in Czech. *Oo*— Yes, what is it now!"

He was no longer addressing Vanessa. Bruno had appeared holding a plate.

"Oh, my food. Right, thanks. I said thanks. No, thanks. Are you sure you're not Czech? No, that's all. No, just leave it. Thanks." Back to Vanessa: "Vanessa, I am not— Or what I mean is, I am— I am a very— Now what are you looking at?"

She gestured toward the window. "I am watching all these people pass. They will see you and me sitting, do you think?"

He did not think. "Look here, Vanessa. No, at me. No one will see us. Everyone's eating at the inn, which is probably why no one eats here. That and the food," he said, shoving his plate away. "And even if someone did see us together, what of it? It wouldn't affect our cover. All they'd think is I had asked you out on a date."

The frigid goddess scoffed. "With a man I am supposed to have never met before this?—a mere handymanning man. Aha! They will think I am a trumpet, then?"

"A 'strumpet,' " Trevor corrected. "You're not a strumpet," he said.

"You only say these things. In my country it is very bad thing to romance with the hired help at the place at which you are visiting. They say it is being the trumpet."

"Yeah? Well, here no one says anything about anybody. And besides, I'm not the hired help, as you well know."

"It is the same, is it not? It is what they are supposed to think that you are, is it not?"

"Not. I mean, yeah. I mean, who cares. Look, Vanessa, if you're too embarrassed to be seen with me——"

"It is not a bare ass. What is this bare ass?"

"Embarrass."

"Ah yes. No, not that. In my country——"

"Yes, I know, they call you a clarinet if you merely look at a man. But we're not in your country, and I'm not——"

"Trevor——" Vanessa was leaning in now, and the hand with which she gripped his was cold and forceful.

"Ouch!" said Trevor, who was finding it a bit too forceful.

"We cannot meet like this." She shot the restauranteur another frown, making sure he was still out of earshot. "You said you had the information."

"I'm not sure I feel like telling you now." Vanessa was not the only one who could act pouty.

"Trevor, try to be sensible. I am supposed to be the well-known artist, and the artist cannot be seen with the——"

"Lowlife handyman," he mumbled—"which I'm not."

"Trevor——"

"And you're no artist," he whispered, almost hissing it.

Vanessa could only frown as Bruno made a visit to their table with the water pitcher. She waited until he had moved on. "I *am* the artist, Trevor. My paintings, they are mine!"

"Really?"

"Of course."

"Didn't know that," he remarked, admiring her all the more for it. "Thought they were, you know, props or something. Neat. You really paint. I tried to fix a fence post this morning," he said, sucking on the end of his thumb. "Didn't go well."

His lunch companion made a sigh of exasperation, and Trevor nodded. There was a time for talking of fence posts, he realized, just as there were moments (he hoped) for bringing up the topic of love. But neither time was now. He could talk business when need-be.

"Listen, I did hear something this morning. From the innkeepers. It's about the murder."

Vanessa was no longer receiving. Twenty meters away, Warren Kingsley, together with Borodin Mahrute and Harvard Blake, had entered the town square.

Warren and Mahrute were talking, while Blake stood staring up at a statue of Colonel Berwald on horseback. (It seemed to him that the animal had an unusual blue tint to it.)

"The bodyguards, they have followed me here!"

"Impossible."

"Yet there they are, Trevor. Your cover at the inn, it remains concealed?"

"Perfectly."

"I think it does not, Trevor. I think it is *pa-fut.*"

"It isn't, I tell you! The guy I took over for up at the inn doesn't know a thing. Besides, he's a frog. I doubt anyone around here can even understand him."

Vanessa was frowning again. Poutingly. "I do not understand this expression frog. He is an amphibian, this person?"

"No, no. I mean, he speaks French. Where I come from, that's what we call them."

"I see. And where you come from, they would be calling me the frog also perhaps?"

"No, no," said Trevor. "They would never do that. They would probably just call you a kraut."

She gave the loiterers another glance. "I think the bodyguards suspect, Trevor."

"Let 'em. They can't prove anything, and from what I can tell, Warren Kingsley is too stupid to even try."

"But what of this Mahrute? I have had experience of his reputation, and he is not stupid."

"No, you're right, he bears watching," said Trevor, remembering that it was Mahrute who had spearheaded the Investigate-Trevor movement. "He's a real pain in the ass, that one."

"Embarrass? How is he embarrass?"

"No, not embarrass… Bare ass. No, not bare ass. He's… It's nothing."

Trevor watched his date. He was shocked to see a smile crease the blusher on her face.

"He is very handsome, this Warren, no?"

"Warren? I don't know. I guess. If you like granite jaws, height and six-pack stomachs."

Vanessa did. "And the other man with them, he is not bad either," she said, running through the roster of male beauty. "Not a total beefcake like the Kingsley, perhaps, but quite nice all the same. Who is this man?"

Trevor was still getting over her beefcake remark. He pulled himself together. "He's just some corporate geek from Redding Enterprises."

He had grown tired of her girlish curiosities. He had become all business now. "If it's not troubling you too much, Vanessa, perhaps we could discuss what I found out this morning. This murder is about to get a lot more sticky," he said, inadvertently placing his hand in the dumplings. He told her all he knew.

It took about five minutes.

Outside the Czech Around Café, Harvard Blake backed off from the statue of Colonel Berwald, no longer interested why his horse looked blue. Unfamiliar with the work of the Jenkins kids, and ignorant of the efforts the town had taken to sandblast away the delinquents' unsolicited brushwork, he simply had to chalk it up to one of those great mysteries, like crop circles or the murder of Thomas Redding. He supposed if Paul Bunyan could have a blue ox named Babe then the colonel had every right to have a bluish animal called (according to the accompanying plaque) Darby. Some relation perhaps.

He walked over to where Mahrute and Warren were standing and twirled his Napoleonic sword at them. "I don't see any sign of Trevor. Sure he came this way?"

Mahrute shook his head.

"Oh well, we'll probably run into him back at the inn fiddling with a reading lamp or something. Never met a handyman more interested in lights and fixtures. He's probably in the lobby mangling a sconce as we speak."

Mahrute agreed that this was always possible. Nevertheless, he preferred to stay on in town until all other alternatives had been explored.

"You don't mind if I take off, do you? It's quite a ways back to my car from here, and I should probably be handing in this sword to someone. Passers-by are already starting to look at me funny. It doesn't put you out trekking back to the inn?"

"Not at all, Mr. Blake. It is not a long walk from here. Thank you for your assistance."

"Anytime," said the sword-wielding PR-meister, and with that, he began his journey back towards Foster country.

"What now?" asked Warren.

Mahrute had decided to shift to Plan B. "Now I would like to talk to the sheriff. His office, I believe, is on the next street over."

Warren said h'm. He had already had enough of Sheriff Ballard to last him the next four vacations and several long weekends. "I think I'll cool my heels in there while you do that." He pointed to an inviting stone archway on the other side of Colonel Berwald's horse. "Looks like some kind of indoor farmer's market going on in there. They might have ginger."

The bodyguards parted shortly thereafter, Mahrute on his errand of professional courtesy, Warren to seek out as much ginger root as he had coming to him. So focused was his path to the market that he failed to notice the wholesome young woman with the light brown hair passing through the archway ahead of him. Had he noticed her, he would have certainly stopped to ask her, once and for all, what she knew about Frederick Luften. (There are some things more important than even lemongrass soup, and meeting up with his mystery woman from the shootout two nights ago was one of them.)

11 – Chairman of the Bored

But their paths did not cross. Nor did Warren's with any ginger. As one self-taught in the gastronomic arts, he didn't know where one grew ginger, what climate it flourished in, or even if it was difficult to cultivate or not. All he knew was he needed it and it was a root, which of course it isn't. It's a rhizome.

Deprived of his simple spice, he moped about the indoor farmer's market, fingering tomatoes and plunking melons. And while there should be no more pleasing task for a young man in the springtime, Warren found this activity unfulfilling. He was about to sidle off when something twenty feet to his left dissuaded him. It wasn't the woman from the shootout, currently standing unseen, twenty feet to his right. It was Judith Carr, arriving through the market's only viable exit to the outside world.

Warren had to think fast. He did not share Harvard Blake's childlike dread of the woman, but he didn't like Judith Carr. He found her tedious and annoying and had never quite gotten over her asking him to carry her presentation board one morning before breakfast. She did not appear to have any presentation boards with her now, but one never knew what she might be hiding under her drooping sweater.

Warren decided not to chance it. He backed away slowly, as many a prospector before him had backed away from a nesting rattle snake.

It was around this time that the woman with the light brown hair noticed him and began backing away herself, like another prospector retreating from a somewhat dull-witted scorpion. She had no desire to run into her chum from the shootout. Spinning on her heel, she moved swiftly through a heavy metal door, this leading into an auditorium.

Warren saw the door himself and followed. He still had not observed his dream woman. Nor had he noticed the prominent sign hanging behind the door:

One Day Only

Judith Carr—"Motivational Movements"

Open Seminar

Judith Carr had not been idle during her enforced stay on the island. Taking advantage of the captive audience, she had set up one of her most dazzling seminars ever, a motivational wonderland, beginning at two p.m. with a speech from the woman herself about seizing the tiny CEO within us all, and ending at four with chips and dip.

The turnout reflected this giddy atmosphere. Primarily left-over Redding Enterprises execs—serious-minded men and women who thought they might be able to get some kind of company credit by attending—there were also a fair share of local yokels, those who had come because they liked the name Judy, or because they liked the concept, or because the mayor was scheduled to say a few words and was always good for a laugh. By five of two, most of the attendees had filtered into the room and taken their seats, some murmuring about the stock market, some about the potato market, others fidgeting in their folding chairs and complaining about bubblegum stuck under the rim. By 2:04, the murmuring and fidgeting had ceased, and everyone had focused their attention at the front of the auditorium.

Well, almost everyone.

A tall, some would say handsome man had slipped in at the last minute, staring around the room, looking for a place to sit. There is always one. Having completed his survey, he was now struggling to make his way to an empty seat in the middle of aisle thirty-five. "Sorry, sorry, sorry. No, my fault. Sorry. Was that your foot?" Reaching it at last, he said, "Oh hey, Peterson. Is this seat taken?", and the executive assistant shook his head.

"Haven't spoken to you since the night of the murder," said Warren, plopping into the chair. It had dawned on him, spotting the little fink from the doorway, that he had hardly seen Eliot Peterson for days, and it's always polite to say Hiya to people. Even if they are finks.

"Looks like I made it in time for the show. What is it, a musical or something? I hope there's dancers. I like dancers."

Eliot Peterson responded with a censuring frown. He was trying to make out the tinny, distorted voice coming from the platform. The speaker, very possibly the mayor, had either said, "Welcome one and all," or "Walking to a bar," and he wanted to hear it.

"Shh," he replied, as the voice began to reflect on Berwald Island history and, if Peterson heard rightly, pinochle. He wasn't the only one having trouble hearing the speech. There appeared to be some sort of technical difficulty with the mic—a hallmark prank of the Jenkins boys, or such was the view of the local yokels.

For a time, there was only mayoral lip service from the stage and the rest was silence, as Hamlet might say.

Warren had seen worse amateur theatre. He turned to Peterson. "I'm pretty new to these things, so let me know if we're supposed to do anything. You know, like cheer or hiss or throw vegetables at the stage. Speaking of which, do you know if they've served any refreshments yet?"

Peterson said he did not. He was trying to listen.

"I guess we got to make the best of it," Warren agreed, pausing to trace the crease in his slacks. "Had these custom made in Milan, you know. Not the creases, just the pants—though I suppose the creases were made there too."

Peterson did not speak. The mayor had mentioned the tragic murder from three nights ago, possibly touching on pinochle, it was difficult to say.

"Someone tried to kill me the other day, you know?" Warren remarked.

"I heard."

"It was pretty exciting."

"I'm sure it was."

"Well, it was," said Warren, who had never cared for sarcasm. It occurred to him why he had avoided Peterson's company up until now. "Any idea what production they're doing?"

"It is not a production, Kingsley. It's a seminar. Judith Carr's seminar."

Warren let out a cry of annoyance. It needed this to make his day complete. No ginger, no ride back to the inn. Just Eliot Peterson and Judith Carr. Perfect.

The muted mayor no longer amused him. Instead, he reminded Warren of those old ghost stories he used to read as a kid, the ones where the ghastly wraith appears, unable to speak of its own demise, but instead hovers there mouthing words of regret. It set the right atmosphere. Slow death by motivational speaking.

It actually reminded Warren of something else he had seen recently. He thought about it a minute and then he had it: the figure in the alley; the guy with the black ski mask and the knife.

Warren finally realized what had been amiss with the encounter. It was the utter silence of the thing. Even when Mahrute was punching the stuffing out of him, he simply stood there quietly and took it. Not a peep. It was like beating up a mime. Why this should have struck Warren as significant, he couldn't say; and then he thought about it some more, and he could say. It was like that with the Kingsley intellect. Throw a few of the right ingredients into the pot, give it a whisk and his deductive powers will eventually come to a boil. For a minute or two of this mental whisking, Warren's inner self flitted away, across the hazy landscape of his mind. He was no longer seated on an uncomfortable chair, jammed in next to an uncomfortable Peterson, watching the mayor of Berwald Island portray a goldfish in a bowl. He was back in the alley, grappling with the mysterious ski-masked marauder. His grip was around the marauder's slender wrist; one of those long, slender legs had just jutted up and clipped him in the jaw with a boot.

A dainty boot. Size 6 at the most.

It was a woman! The ski-masked marauder had been a woman! That's why she had kept her moans and groans to herself. Secrecy and silence. Pretty tough broad, whoever she was. Warren doubted that he could have kept his feelings to himself in that situation; and he was a big strong bodyguard. He was astounded.

He might have shared his breakthrough with Peterson, but the assistant most likely wouldn't have appreciated the subtlety. It wasn't the appropriate moment anyhow. One of the Redding Enterprises AV geeks had gotten the mic working again and the mayor had finished his off-color joke and left the platform. Judith Carr had taken the stage.

Eliot Peterson gave her his full attention. He was one of her more ardent fans, which did not speak well for either one of them.

Warren continued to twitch in his seat. He was getting antsier by the minute. As the meeting unfolded he tried to amuse himself. He glanced absently about the room: first at the ceiling; then at the floor; then, as time drew on, at his pants, at his shoes, at the ceiling again, and briefly into the whicker handbag belonging to an elderly woman on his left. Finding little among these to hold his interest, he turned his attention to the opposite aisle, where a wholesome woman with light brown hair was seated some rows down. This wholesome, attractive woman fascinated Warren strangely and he suddenly realized why.

"It's her!" he gasped, speaking to no one at first; then turning and directing the comment at Peterson. "That's the girl!" he repeated. "Not the one in the ski mask, but the nice one, in the tan trench coat. The one from the shooting!"

The clarification did little to enliven Eliot Peterson. He glanced over at the woman, nodded, and turned his attention back to the stage.

"We've been looking everywhere for her!" said Warren. "Actually, we totally forgot about her, but there she is." He leaned over (apologizing for elbowing the elderly woman with the handbag) and went "PSST!"

This met with mixed results.   Two men turned around and scowled, and a woman sitting beside them asked the man sitting in front of her if he could hear something leaking.

Warren gave it another try.   "Hey…" he huffed, in a hushed tone. "Hey…"

When this failed to bring home the goods, he threw a pencil at her. When this hit a bald man, he decided to go with something less subtle. "HEY!"

The woman frowned and looked behind her.   At first, she couldn't make out what all the commotion was about. All around her, the audience appeared to be writhing. People were grumbling, men were rubbing their heads and women were clenching their handbags.   Then, in the midst of the chaos, she spotted Warren, bobbing up and down in his seat, arms waving.

She froze.

"We've been looking everywhere for you," Warren uttered, sending another bristle through the audience. "We need to talk!"

The woman stared.

"So how are you? No bullet holes from the other night, I hope?"

The woman blinked.

"It's great running into you like this.   We should go somewhere and chat. No, you stay there. Catch you after the conference," he remarked, amidst a chorus of shushes.

The woman continued to stare. She hadn't spoken; she hadn't moved. She only blinked. Blinked and stared.

"Meet me in the farmer's market," Warren went on, acknowledging a stern request from the seminar moderator, now at his side. "You know, after the formalities here."

The seminar moderator, now joined by a cadre of Redding AV geeks, explained that the gentleman would have to keep quiet if the gentleman wanted to remain at the seminar.

Warren said the gentleman didn't care one way or the other, but as long as his lady friend was sticking around, he was too. He would keep quiet now, thanks.

Silence.

"Actually, on second thought, meet me in the lobby," he yelled twenty seconds later. "They might have refreshments. Not out front, behind the…"

Fifteen seconds later, Warren Kingsley came twirling out the door into the market. He was followed shortly by his so-called lady friend, asking someone offstage to kindly take their hands off her. Some moments after that came Eliot Peterson, who had more cause for complaint than either one of them.

"But I was just sitting there!" he said.

The Redding AV geeks did not tolerate backchat. Straightening their ties and short sleeve shirts, they turned and slammed the door of the auditorium behind them.

Peterson harrumphed. He had never been ejected from a motivational speaking seminar before and he didn't like it. "Open these doors immediately," he shouted, banging the metal. He spun around and glared at the source of his premature exit. "HR will hear about this," he told them.

Once he had flounced off, the woman turned and looked at Warren. Warren looked back at her.

"You haven't seen any ginger around here, have you?" he asked.

12 – STRANGE COMPANY

When two new acquaintances are reunited, most notably two acquaintances who have recently fled gunfire together, it can be difficult getting the confab rolling again. Conversation fizzles. This is especially true if one party—let us call her X—would rather that they wrap this up briskly so she and the second party—for the sake of argument, Y—can get on with their separate lives as soon as possible.

Y was not entirely ignorant of this distinction. You'd have to be a pretty thick customer—well, thicker than Y—not to pick up on the hints. And Y—let us call him Warren—had already detected a certain aloofness in his fellow exile. He decided to play it cool himself. "Sorry for the ruckus," he told her, as they strolled past the cucumbers and squash, "just wanted your attention."

"Well, you got it," she said.

There was no warmth in her reply. Warren congratulated himself on choosing the cool and detached route. You can't overdo the cool, detached thing. "It's pleasant running into you like this," he went on. "I mean, it's nice. Very nice. Running into you like this," he clarified.

He paused. There was something unmistakably uncool about that last run of speech, he realized. Not entirely detached either. "I mean, if you like that sort of thing," he said.

"If I like what sort of thing?" she wondered.

"Never mind," he answered. "Hey, you never told me your name."

"Maybe that's for the best."

"Right," said Warren. Anonymous. The only way. "You already know my name. It's Warren, in case you've forgotten. Warren Kingsley. But you must have heard of me?"

"Not before this weekend."

"Ah," he said. This was why it was so important that people spelled your name right in the newspaper. "Well, as you probably know, I'm a very famous bodyguard, which is no doubt why you contacted me in the first place?"

"You're a bodyguard?"

Warren was definitely feeling depressed now. "You didn't know?"

"I knew you worked for Tom—for Thomas Redding." She paused, tracing her fingers over a yellow gourd. It looked a little like Tom Redding. "It doesn't matter now."

"But what about Frederick Luften?"

She stopped to dab an eyelash from her lid. Unlike Vanessa Skinner, she wore very little eye makeup, which Warren Kingsley appreciated.

"Do you like your job?" she asked.

Warren considered this.

"I guess I do. It's all right. It's not very difficult. All you have to do is look tough most of the time. Sometimes you have to get involved in things, but even then it's usually nothing more than pouncing on some thugs, sitting on their chests and telling them to keep very still until the police arrive. Pretty easy."

"Sitting on their chests?"

"And telling them to keep very still until the police arrive."

"And then your client thanks you brokenly and gives you a huge raise?"

"Actually my client is usually dead by that point. But I suppose, in theory, he could thank me, yes." He showed her the way out into the town square, keeping a careful eye cocked for anyone on whose chest he might have to sit on her behalf. "How about your job?"

"I liked it once."

"But not now?"

"I've been kept away from it. I guess there's no one for me to sit on about it."

"You just have to keep looking. In my experience, there's always someone or something standing in your way. If there is, I recommend you pounce on them and throttle them into submission."

"Until the police arrive?"

"Until your kudos arrive. And your just due. That's what I say. Just pounce and sit."

This seemed to be Warren's recipe for everything, she said. Pouncing and sitting.

"It usually is. Hey! Do you like soup?"

"The last time we spoke you asked me if I liked cod."

"Now I'm asking you if you like soup. Do you?"

"It's all right."

"Not this soup. It's spectacular!"

"You will have to treat me to it sometime. Meanwhile, I should be going."

"But you haven't told me about Luften."

"There is no Luften," she sighed.

Warren was resolute. "Look, I know you don't think it's important—"

"You don't understand," said the woman, looking past Warren and frowning. She placed a hand on his face, sending a jolt of ecstasy through his rugged frame. "There is no Frederick Luften," she whispered. "There never was."

And with these parting words, the woman vanished. Warren couldn't help noticing that she was doing a lot of that lately.

Borodin Mahrute joined him. "Was that the young lady from the shooting?"

Warren said it was. "Leaving because she spotted you, Mahrute, thank you very much."

"I am sorry."

Sorry didn't get Warren buxom brunettes with large, luminous eyes. He rested his palm where hers had so recently lain. "She was telling me that there is no Frederick Luften. I'm trying to decide if she was being whimsical or not."

"Perhaps not," Mahrute replied. "I spoke with the sheriff and he—"

"Not now," said Warren. "My mind isn't on what you're saying. And I want to be focused, because it sounds like it's going to make my head throb, whatever it is. By the way, speaking of heads, I saw

Trevor Green's tiny one bobbing off into the distance a little while ago."

"When was this?"

"Shortly after you left to talk to Ballard. He was skulking off in the same direction as Harvey Blake. Didn't seem important at the time."

Warren Kingsley, in his whimsical way, might have described Trevor as skulking after Blake, but in Trevor's opinion he would have said it was more like staggering, both physically and spiritually. Physically, because at some point in his travels he had picked up a piece of brick from a construction site and this was throwing off his equilibrium. Spiritually, because moments before leaving the Czech Around Café, the lady in his life, Vanessa Skinner, had asked him if he wouldn't mind terribly battering Harvard Blake over the head with it.

She hadn't specified the brick—as an artist herself, she left the blunt object in question open to personal interpretation. And she hadn't demanded death—not in a Roman colosseum, thumbs-down sense. There was no reason that Blake had to end up like Thomas Redding. They simply needed a distraction, she explained, something to keep the state police busy while she and Trevor continued their plans at the inn. If the faux handyman was correct, and Ballard's days were numbered as chief inspector on the Redding investigation, then the arrival of the police, the real police, was certainly imminent. Like a kitten—or *kocka*—with a ball of yarn these police must be given something to divert their attentions. Harvard Blake was the obvious choice. He was a suspect in the Redding murder, and for him to disappear—cold-cocked and tied up in the trunk of his car—the authorities would have no choice but to go look for him. Suspicion would shift. The inn and all the guests in it would hold no fascination—for a time, at any rate—and a time was all Vanessa needed. Much of her plans were already in progress. All she required was someone to tie up the loose ends for her. And with these loose ends, Harvard Blake.

She hadn't insisted that Trevor accept her nomination. Vanessa never insisted. She merely pointed out that if he wanted her to entertain his offer to develop their relationship past the professional, then he would need to perform these occasional chores for her. She asked very little of her suitors, really.

Trevor Green had learned a lot about becoming a Vanessa-man today. He wouldn't have thought it possible, but he actually longed for those Arcadian moments between the watercress and the coffee. Those carefree minutes when his only concern was that Vanessa considered Warren a bit of a beefcake. The brick placed a whole new complexion on the matter.

Trevor didn't do the rough stuff. Since coming to Connecticut he had forsaken his ethics, subjugated his ego and accepted employment under false pretenses. But this was different. Beating people over the head with bricks had a violent tinge to it. Trevor didn't do the violence. Yet he wanted Vanessa, and Vanessa meant violence. Doing one meant doing the other. It was one of those grand dilemmas philosophers have been wrestling with for centuries. Trevor would have to make his decision carefully, for there was no turning back once he had. He knew this, yet still he staggered forward.

He could think a lot clearer once he had stuffed Blake in the trunk.

Blake had no inkling of the flanneled, brick-wielding figure lurking behind him. As he ambled along the deserted backstreets, he inhaled the salt air and whistled. He had started with Vivaldi's "Four Seasons," probably because someone at the inn had been listening to it on the radio the other evening; but he was a mercurial whistler at heart and had now shifted to a Dave Brubeck medley. It was the whistling that allowed him to be tracked with such ease.

He had just wrapped up a few details in his mind regarding Warren and a soup gala for the mayor, when he arrived at the cobblestone street where he had parked his car and slowed his ambling to an amiable trot.

In general, Blake was a man of high principles. When he set his mind to work, he typically stuck to it without distraction. But there was something that obsessed him outside his gift of PR, something from which not even the charm of fraternizing with bodyguards or seeking suspicious handymen could dissuade him. It was his addiction; his recreation; the Vanessa Skinner to his Trevor, the mystery woman to his Warren Kingsley.

It was his car, a Jaguar XJR.

He had bought it at auction awhile back, and although it wasn't his habit to splurge in this manner—he wasn't what you would call a materialist, not in the purest sense—he wasn't ashamed to say that he loved the thing.

And the Jag loved him. Yes, they had their share of squabbles, akin to what is experienced by supermodels when they go slumming with handsome shoe salesmen. (After the momentary thrill has worn off, both parties begin to come to their senses and it becomes clear that she has linked her life with someone below her.)

That not withstanding, it was a fast car, and it was his.

He approached the vehicle with a smile, its champagne frame glistening—well, not in the sun, because there wasn't any right now—but in the haze. After his roller-coaster afternoon, the only thing he was looking forward to was sliding back in between its limited edition leather seats. He drifted up to the door, still whistling: and it was with a sudden mangling of the chorus of "Light My Fire," that he discovered that his baby was sitting atop four cement blocks; these blocks most certainly provided by the hoodlums who had borrowed the four special issue, alloy racing wheels.

He stood there goggling. He would not have known it, but this boyish peccadillo actually represented the second Jenkins prank he had encountered that day. First the blue statue in the town square, and now this. Recognizing this as the rather amusing coincidence that it was might have eased the sting somewhat, though probably not, and it didn't matter anyway, because he didn't recognize it. He just goggled.

Behind him, concealed behind a plastic model of a giant tuna, Trevor Green also goggled. This was an unforeseen development. He had finally manned himself for the bashing and the trunking, but what good did it do bashing the man, if the car trunk required was sitting on top of four cement blocks. Even the Berwald Island police could track down a fugitive lying in a trunk in an immobilized Jaguar.

He would have to improvise. He had promised his woman he would do the deed, and like a tiny-headed Macbeth he stepped out from the tuna to do it. He could figure out what to do with the body later (perhaps Blake, who seemed to know the island better than he did, would have a suggestion).

He had gotten as far as cocking his brick back, at which point his victim shifted in place, causing the sunlight to gleam off the Napoleonic sword entrusted to his care.

Trevor gasped and zigged awkwardly off in the opposite direction, keeping his face concealed from view. He tried whistling but what came out was no Vivaldi.

Vanessa hadn't mentioned anything about swords. The ethics of bashing people over the head took yet another turn in Trevor's thoughts. He would have to brood on them for a while.

It was just as well. A few seconds earlier Blake had pressed the little button on his keychain which controlled the Jag's handy car alarm. He pressed it again now. CHIRP. And once more. CHIRP-CHIRP. Still no tires.

He was thinking what to do next, having exhausted the most obvious choices, when a car horn sounded behind him. HOOT. He looked down at the remote inquisitively. He hadn't remembered it making that noise before.

HOOT-HOOT repeated the horn.

The mists cleared, and Blake discovered an antique Toyota Land Cruiser idling in the lane beside him. At the wheel was a woman, somewhat familiar looking but he couldn't quite place her. She appeared to be hooting at him.

"Someone swiped your tires," she observed.

Blake agreed that someone had.

"Well, it's no good pressing that thing," she remarked.

Blake followed her eyes to the keychain. He supposed it wasn't—any good pressing it.

"So do you need a ride or what?" she asked.

Blake supposed he did. He jumped in, and Warren's unnamed dream woman, fresh from her meeting with the bodyguard in the town square, toed the gas pedal and they were off.

13 – WORKPLACE POLITICS

"**Y**ou don't remember me, do you?" she asked, creaking up Old Meadow Brook Lane.

"I do," claimed Harvard Blake. "I remember you distinctly. La—"

"Are you singing?"

"I'm saying your name, which, as we all know, begins with a La sound."

"Loren," said the woman.

"Well, it's a sort of La sound," he argued. "It's great to see you again, Loren. We were in high school together, weren't we?"

"And elementary school. And briefly kindergarten, before you freed Mrs. Gregory's hamsters and they stuck you in the class with the tough kids."

"Those gerbils were going over the wall whether I assisted or not," said Harvard Blake.

"But you stirred them up; spoke to their inner-gerbil. I remember admiring you for it at the time... The ponytail is new, isn't it?"

"Fairly new, yes."

"And only about fifteen years out of date. Still, it's nice to see a man who doesn't trim his hair down to the nub." She steered the Land Cruiser onto a tiny backroad. What the residents called Old Old Meadow Brook Lane. "Ever make it to Yale?"

"I did. Best six months of my life."

"And from there, not onto—"

"No, I stalwartly avoided my namesake, not that they would have had me at that point."

"I'm sure someone could have swung it for you."

"Now that you mention it, there was some talk of grandpapa pulling some strings, dedicating another library, something of that sort, but I quietly applied to a nice country college behind their backs and slipped away in the night. I had to have some revenge for my parents saddling me with this moniker."

"I've always liked it," said Loren, with an abrupt frown. She chewed her bottom lip.

Decidedly girly that last statement. And girliness was exactly what she wasn't after. Sure, there had been a time, back when she was the one with the ponytail and he was never seen anywhere without a toy phaser, that she had cared for Harvard Blake, moniker and all. Cared for him from afar. But even if that crush had thrived well into high school, what did that have to do with now? Despite what most chick flicks would have you believe, women can grow out of their girlish fancies. Their younger selves might sit dreaming about showering their idol with kisses, or—according to personal preference—ruling over the hamster kingdom together—but despite these lush romantic notions, emotions can fade with age.

Loren knew that Harvard had never paid her the slightest attention all those years ago. She was an adult now, and she had no reason to believe that Harvard the man felt any differently about her than Harvard the boy. They were and always had been just friends.

"What did you say?" she asked, having realized that Harvard the man had just asked her a question.

"I said, did you wind up at Juilliard?"

"Oh. Yeah, I ended up at Juilliard all right."

"And?"

"Picture the Harvard Blake story, substitute female lead."

"Right," he said, bobbing up and down in his seat as the Land Cruiser clawed and scraped its way to the peak of Old Old Meadow Brook. "Life's roads are seldom smoothly paved, are they? Nor, for that matter, are Berwald Island's," he added.

The word road touched a chord with Loren. She laughed. "I never asked you where you were going!"

Blake, who considered replying "down the drain," realized that they had switched from the metaphysical to the literal. "Berwald Island Inn. It's— Well, as a matter of fact, I have no clue where it is. You seem to have dragged us off into the backwoods, Loren, like murderers do in all your better B-horror movies. You're not the Berwald Island strangler, are you?"

Loren did not reply. She might have been the Berwald Island strangler asked an especially awkward question. "You're staying at the inn?"

"Is that a problem?"

"No. No, of course not. Not at all."

"Oh good," said Blake, relieved. "Are you at a hotel too? I assume you still make your home in Boston?"

"I'm staying with family," she answered abruptly. Maybe a little too abrupt.

"That's right, you used to have an aunt and uncle in Connecticut, didn't you?"

"Still do," she said, grinding the gears of the transmission. "You remembered that?"

Harvard said of course he did. He used to envy their proximity to Foxwoods Casino, he remarked.

Loren gave a wry smile. She should have known that there would be a sensible reason. "Right," she replied, twisting the steering wheel as if it had been a certain childhood friend's outdated ponytail.

Blake was confused. The atmosphere had changed in the car. Something he had said or done had ticked her off. It couldn't simply be his constant, unmanly jiggling in the seat. Plenty of good men through the ages, he was sure, had jiggled around in antique Land Cruisers. She hadn't even provided him a seatbelt.

Then he saw it. He had been a total idiot.

The inn! The murder of Thomas Redding. "You probably read about it, and here I am babbling about Berwald Island stranglers. It must have struck you as pretty crass. You did read about it, I take it?"

Loren confessed to hearing something or other about a murder.

"I knew that must be it."

"Did you know him?" she asked. "The murdered man?"

"Old Redding? If anyone could ever truly know that sociopathic skinflint. I guard my words, having always been taught to speak well of the dead. He was my boss."

"You sound happy someone killed him."

"Happy? No, not happy. Warm and content maybe, but not happy. I'm not a proponent of murder, but if there ever was a can-tankerous old fool whose sole mission in life was to make everyone else's life miserable, it was he. A golf club to the back of the skull could only improve him. Did you say something?"

Loren hadn't. She had muttered "You bet!" but it was only a passing thought.

"Anyway, let's not talk about the Redding murder," he said. "It's all in the past now, like our respective scholastic careers."

Loren couldn't agree more. "Anyway, I did it."

Blake didn't follow. For a moment—

Then seeing they were stopped, he looked out the window and smiled. "The Berwald Island Inn!"

"As promised. I told you I'd get you back in one piece and I did it."

"Amazing," said Blake, climbing out. He stumbled slightly on the way down, but plenty of good men have stumbled. "You know all the shortcuts, don't you? Come in for a cup of cocoa or a corn chowder or something?"

"You're the second man to ask me to soup today," she said. It made her feel all tingly inside, these offers. "I'm gonna pass. I should be getting back."

"Maybe I'll see you around, then? Allow me to thank you prop-erly?"

"You can always try," Loren agreed, and drove cheerfully away.

She continued driving for about fifty yards—around the back of the inn, past a grove of pine trees, and onto a narrow gravel drive-way, out of view of Blake. She got out and walked across the gravel to the hotel.

The first person she encountered inside was the innkeeper Ches-ter, coming out of the kitchen.

"Hiya, Uncle Chet."

"Hiya, Loren." His eyes lit up, but there was a sense of concern behind the gleam. "You should watch yourself down here, honey.

Redding's people are all over the place. One of them might recognize you."

"I know. I'm being careful, don't worry."

"I thought you agreed to stay in your room."

"I just went out for some air. Girls need their air."

"You're in one of your silly moods, I see."

"Just a little. Looks like you're in one of yours too. You have grease on your cheek, Uncle Chet."

"Do I?" He attended to the matter, rubbing in a circular motion and forming the smudge into a little lake of soot. "Must have happened while I was out. I bought some new tires today."

"Tires?"

"From the Jenkins kids. Who says they're all bad, huh?"

He went on to explain how he had been tooling around town earlier and they had waved him over and sold him the things in an alley behind Nick Foster's place.

"Alloy racing wheels. For a C-note. Installed them on my Le Sabre and everything. I wonder how they can afford to sell stuff so cheap."

"Low overhead?" she offered, and Chester said it must be something like that.

Loren might have looked happy, but inside she groaned in spirit. She felt bad for poor Harvard, going through life wheel-less, and yet she couldn't bring herself to dampen her uncle's enthusiasm. He was taking a great risk letting her stay here. The least she could do was allow him his simple pleasures. And Harvard could certainly afford to buy new tires.

She followed her uncle across the hall into his office.

"You shouldn't be wandering around like this," he was saying. "I was telling your aunt this morning that we can't keep you concealed here forever. Not with the sheriff's office making its typical hash of the investigation, and the state police—"

The words died on his lips.

Chester was standing on the threshold of his office, bowled over by something on the other side of the door. The discovery of another bludgeoned tycoon could hardly have affected him with more drama.

"Loren, a gigantic shrub appears to have sprouted up on my desk."

Loren thought it might have. "I know. The herb people put it there."

"Who are the herb people?"

"They're herb people. People who deal in herbs. Family by the name of Benson. They bought Berwald farm last year. They came here today and peppered the inn with vegetation. Herbs, veggies, various treats like that. It must have been while you were out buying your tires."

"But why is my desk peppered? My desk was nice enough without pepper."

"Aunt Deirdre said it's for the soups the new chef is making. She said something about his personal manager ordering it all, which is weird, because I didn't think chefs had managers."

"And why can't he manage his ingredients elsewhere? What did I ever do to this man?"

Loren might have answered that he had bought his alloy racing wheels from the Jenkins boys; but as no one had bothered to tell her that the chef's new manager was her old school friend Harvard, she could only shake her head and say something about karma.

Chester, who thought karma was a kind of cookie, said, "What is all this junk?"

"Let's see. That there is cilantro. On the floor is basil. And unless I miss my guess the little fellow peeking out from the filing cabinet is fennel."

"How nice."

"They're just herbs, Uncle Chet. They won't bite."

He eyed the leafy specimens rudely. It was as though his office had become the set for some sci-fi flick, the episode where the ship is overrun by alien vegetation. "But I don't want herbs," he complained, "biting or otherwise. My office is nothing but fennel now. Fennel and cilantro and parsley and sage."

"You sounded like Simon and Garfunkel there. Shall I fetch my tambourine?"

Chester was not in the mood. "You were here, Loren. Why didn't you tell them to put this stuff in the kitchen?"

"Not enough afternoon sunlight. Plants need their sun. Your office has the perfect window, making it an ideal—though tiny—greenhouse."

The word tiny said it all. The Oxford English people, giving the place the once over, would have concluded that it missed the definition of office by several yards. In reality, it was more of a cubby. Just enough space for a desk (now foliaged-up) and a waste basket.

Chester kicked this waste basket petulantly. "This is outrageous! I'm calling these herb people and having them pick up their demon seeds this minute. Who wants fresh soups anyway? We can go back to cup-a-noodle as far as I'm concerned."

"It's up to you. Aunt Deirdre won't like it."

Chester replied that he didn't care what Aunt Deirdre liked or disliked, and muttered something disparaging about her which involved fennel plants.

"And the same goes for this Stanford Busby, or whatever his name is."

Loren stared. "Do you mean Harvard Blake?"

"That's right. The chef's manager."

"He's the chef's manager?"

"Yes. Manager to Chef Warren. Who ever heard of a bodyguard making soup?"

Loren stared again. "Warren Kingsley is the new chef?"

"Yes. Why do you keep jumping like that? You made me breathe in a whiff of fennel the wrong way."

Loren was beginning to feel overexposed.

"I think maybe you were right, Uncle Chet. I'll be heading back to my little corner now. Am I likely to run into anyone on the way?"

Chester shook his head. "We moved everyone's accommodations to the other side of the inn. The police asked us to keep the rooms around the crime scene clear, so if you go that way I doubt anyone will see you."

"The rooms around the crime scene are clear?"

"With strips of yellow tape everywhere," said Chester, who was considering marking up his tiny office the same way.

His niece thanked him, surreptitiously slipping an object off the hook on the door as she did so. It might not have been the most gracious way to repay her uncle's hospitality, swiping his master key while he wasn't looking, but as the Jenkins boys would attest, it's okay if you're only borrowing it.

In a room on the other side of the hotel, Harvard Blake sat thinking about his old friend Loren. It's funny how seeing someone you haven't met in years can boost your spirits so readily. The tire incident had bummed him for sure, but he had hardly given the special alloys another thought on the ride back. Then again, Loren always had been a great girl. One of the world's real life forces. It bothered him that everything wasn't going right for her—he wondered what her little troubles were—and then he sighed, feeling somewhat bummed again. Coming full circle, as it were.

At this point in his reflections, the tiny orchestra playing on his mobile phone's speaker took a breather, and a monotone voice broke in on his daydream, "How can I help you." Blake picked up.

"Hi, credit department? Hi. I have a card with your company. What? No, it's fine. I was wondering what sort of replacement deals you offer on merchandise. See, I bought some tires with your card a little while ago and someone swiped them. No, my deductible is too high with them. I thought your company might cover something like this. Exactly. So you don't do anything like that? The reason why I ask is I saw this commercial once where some kid busts his new toy, and you replaced it. In the commercial. What's that? No, I don't remember. Race car or something. No, mine's full size. So I just thought… Right. Exactly. Thanks anyway." He replaced the receiver.

That settled the tire issue.

From outside in the hallway he could hear a sound not unlike a tall, chiseled man whining under his breath. Perhaps he, too, had been deprived of his alloy racing wheels.

Blake went to the door and observed Warren and Mahrute passing, a two-man personal security parade. "You guys got back in one piece this time, I see?"

Mahrute agreed that they had.

"Heading somewhere?"

Mahrute conceded that they were.

"Want any company?" asked Blake. He wanted to take his mind off things.

The bodyguards proved the perfect diversion. According to Mahrute, they were on their way to examine Thomas Redding's room—although if you had asked Warren there was no point. The Berwald Island police had already been all over the place. They might not be CSI Connecticut, but they still knew how to study a crime scene. Snooping around now was a waste of everybody's time, time that could be better spent explaining to the inn's kitchen staff why you don't add uncooked flour to a cream-based stock.

They arrived at the door, and Mahrute paused to feel around in the pocket of his waistcoat. The sheriff, he said, had given him a copy of the pass key.

"Don't need it," Warren told them, turning the handle. "Door's already open."

They went in.

The satisfaction of showing up his peer diminished slightly as Warren tripped over the edge of the area rug inside the room and careened into a Tiffany tea set.

All the carpets in the inn were of an identical size and pattern—Deirdre liked consistency—but something about the carpet in his late employer's room was always tripping Warren up, causing him to barge into tea sets or whatever else happened to be in his path. Last time it had been a semi-nude water nymph by Pollaiuolo.

The Pollaiuolo in the corner and the tea set on the floor was only a small part of the old man's collection. All around them ranged antiquities of every description.

There was antique mahogany, ancient porcelain and old-time art deco.

One observed nymphs, both nude and strangely inhibited; busts of historical figures no one had ever heard of; and soapstone carvings of goggle-eyed woodland creatures nobody ever liked.

There were artifacts from the eighteenth century, from the nineteenth century and a few that may well have come from the twenty-second century, brought back in time.

The tycoon had pulled in an impressive haul on his trip. In fact, had some uppity member of his acquaintance not bludgeoned him to death with an antique golf club, it was likely a cascade of vintage newspapers or old Coke bottles would have eventually done the job on the murderer's behalf.

Blake stood soaking in the surroundings with a sneer. He had never understood his employer's fetish for history's junkyard. Blake's sole concession to the past was his ponytail, which, as his friend Loren had pointed out, only dated back to the early 1990s.

Mahrute was examining a statue in the center of the room. Like its subject matter, it commanded respect, despite its size. "Would this be the statue Mr. Redding had delivered the night of his murder?"

Blake nodded. "That's it."

Mahrute continued to study it. He attempted to lift it and set it back down. Warren had been correct, it wasn't light. They made their Napoleons solid in Berwald Island.

"I guess this relic was Redding's last purchase," said Blake. "That, and King Kong's stogie over there." He nodded toward a small, tightly wrapped carpet, about three feet in length. He remembered it had also arrived the night of the murder. He one-handed it and waggled it gently, as if tempted to say there was nothing like a good cigar.

He squinted into the tube. "I wonder if the old guy even looked at this rug before he bought it. Probably not. Let's do him the honor, shall we?" He untied and flicked the miniature runner into the air, watching as it snapped to its full length and hit Warren in the head.

"Hey! Knock that off!" he said. He was getting tired of life pelting him with antiques.

Blake was too busy scowling over the pattern to take any notice of Warren's protests. Paisley print, very worn and far too many fleurs-de-lis for his tastes. "Crap," he considered it, and moved on. He continued his tour with the water nymphs in the corner.

Warren had yet to move past the Napoleon. "Still got a kink in my back from lugging this, you know," he told Mahrute. "All Peterson got was a few rug burns. Although why Harvey thinks that tiny runner—" He paused. "Did you squeak, Mahrute?"

Mahrute said he hadn't. He wouldn't even know how.

"I heard it too," Blake remarked, reluctantly taking a break from the nymphs.

"It's coming from this crate," said Warren, pinpointing the sound.

Mahrute lifted the lid.

In all fairness to Warren Kingsley, many men, jabbed in the stomach by a figure rapidly exiting a crate with its head down, would have toppled over, grasping their abs, unable to move. And in defense of Harvard Blake, many men prompted with the sight of a figure head-butting their friend in the stomach would have sprung backwards and squealed like a little girl.

One should not judge either one of them.

In any event, with his client down for the count and his client's personal promoter having a fit of the vapors, it was left to Mahrute to give chase.

He needn't have bothered. The figure began by bouncing off the antique mahogany, continued by upsetting the ancient porcelain, and finally stumbled over the old-time art deco. It had made it as far as the door when it met up with the newly arrived gut of Sheriff Ballard. Officer and suspect went down in a tangle, and that was how Mahrute found them: a pile of arms and legs, lying in the hallway.

Warren and Blake caught up to them half-a-minute later.

"Loren!" said Blake, goggling down at his old school friend.

"Loren?" asked Warren, recognizing his heretofore unnamed Luften source (and dream woman).

"Loren honey?" gasped Sheriff Ernest Ballard, pulling away from the heap.

"Loren honey?" asked Warren again, annoyed that everyone seemed to know this woman's label but him.

Loren climbed to her feet and gave them all a smile, not as dazzling as it had once been, but not bad with the wind knocked out of her.

"Hiya, Uncle Ernie," was all she said.

14 – BOTTOM LINE

"**I** guess this is the part where I toss up my hands and say where do I begin?" she remarked, once the five of them had settled inside her room. "Boy, where do I begin," she asked, not actually tossing up her hands but sitting on the edge of the bed with a sort of hand-tossing moan. She looked at the four faces staring down at her. If it weren't for the soothing presence of her uncle, the lawman, she might have been a lady of the evening whose services had been overbooked.

"Try starting with your name," said Warren, still feeling like he was several chapters behind the rest of the class. He felt that way a lot.

"You're Loren Hamilton," answered Mahrute, and once again Warren snorted. Did he miss a conference call or something? "I didn't recognize you in town the other evening," the bodyguard's bodyguard explained. "You wore your hair differently on your CD."

"She has a CD?" asked Warren, even more bewildered.

Loren managed another smile. "So you're the one who bought it?"

"I am sure you are just being modest."

"You streamed it off the Internet, didn't you? It's okay, I'm not in it for the royalties."

Blake noticed the violin lying on the dressing table. He picked it up, cradling it with slightly more care than he would have shown a newborn chick. "It was you I heard playing the other night. Vivaldi and Bach and something else that may or may not have been Haydn. I thought it was the radio."

"Crackly and monotone you mean?"

"It was beautiful!"

"Tell that to the Bath Chamber Orchestra. They fired me."

"What! Someone ought to beat their brains in with a French horn," said Blake, and then remembering Sheriff Ballard and the murder investigation, added, "which is to say, someone should send them a strongly worded note asking them to reconsider their decision. Why did they fire you?"

"It wasn't their fault. Tom Redding made them do it. He wanted to get back at me."

"What's the old coot got to do with it? Get back at you for what?"

"Divorcing him. Or marrying him, depending on how you look at it."

For a brief shining moment Warren Kingsley was no longer the only one in the room lacking in the latest Loren news. Her declaration that she had once been intimate with a man who looked (and behaved) like a dissipated gargoyle had stunned them all equally.

The sheriff found words first. "Thomas Redding was the man Dee-Dee told me about? The man you secretly married and divorced last summer?"

"It only lasted about four months," she said. "Only two months shorter than Harvard's visit to Yale."

Blake shh-ed her with mild reproach. He didn't like these things getting around. Not good for his street cred as a PR guru.

Ballard persisted, "But, honey, how could you? Redding? He was old enough to be—"

"You had to see him in a tuxedo, Uncle Ernie. He was a totally different man in a tuxedo. He used to come to our performances when he was in town on business. I won't say we fell in love or anything—no sense contributing to everybody's heebie-jeebies—but we got comfortable around each other. I don't know, for a time we gave each other what we needed. And then we didn't, and the marriage went down like it was drilled in the back of the head by an 3-2 fastball."

"You like baseball?" asked Blake, still experiencing the heebies, but pretty well situated regarding the jeebies.

"I don't mind watching the occasional game," said Loren, and Blake smiled. He had never known a girl who liked baseball.

"But you were saying something about someone plunking your marriage?"

"We both plunked it. We plunked it hard. Eventually we went our separate ways. It was either that or kill each other. Sorry, bad choice of words. Everything would have been fine, too, but then someone gave Tom some bad advice, and that's when things got ugly."

Warren had a question. He had blanked out there for a couple minutes, wondering what the difference was between a violin and a viol, but he had floated back to the surface now.

"So what were you doing in the crate?" he asked.

He knew musicians did some weird things to improve acoustics, but this was a first. Perhaps it was something unique to violinists, though possibly not violists.

"We opened the lid and out you popped like a Jack in the box."

Loren had a simple enough explanation for that. "I heard you all coming and hid. The crate seemed the most obvious place."

"So you were in the room the whole time we were?"

"I was. You know, Warren, if this bodyguarding thing doesn't work out, you have a real future as a detective. Great powers of deduction."

"I'll stick with the soup thanks," he said, preferring to leave the PI stuff to Mahrute. "But why? Why were you even in the same hotel with Redding? You weren't trying to reconcile, were you?"

It was actually a pretty good question, and one Loren would have preferred Warren hadn't asked. She liked him better when his questions were insipid and cloth-headed. "Yeah. The thing is, I came here to confront him over our settlement."

"You wanted more money?" asked Blake, almost more shocked by this than he was over her marriage to a gargoyle.

"Don't make it sound so sordid. Originally I wasn't going to ask for anything in the divorce. I was more than happy to treat the whole thing like a long, bad vacation. But then the orchestra canned me, and I did a little snooping and learned that Tom, one of its primary benefactors, had had me fired. And not only that, he had bad-mouthed me to every orchestra who would listen. I couldn't prove anything, so I talked to a lawyer and he said if I wanted to get any of my own back I had no choice but to seek some money in the divorce. It was almost as if Tom wanted me to come after him that way, and it was the last thing I wanted, really. But I was angry and the lawyer had this woeful look in his eye, like he was about to miss a Mercedes payment, and I decided the hell with it, we might as well tackle the Redding millions.

"Only, there weren't any. My head still swims when I think about it, but once we got everything out in the open, it appeared that Tom had very few liquid assets. I was entitled to a pittance in alimony, and if I really worked at it I could have gotten a portion of his collection, which didn't suit me at all. You can't live on antique curios. Tom's attorneys had already branded me as a gold-digger, so I didn't have the arbiter's sympathies. Tom's net worth was taken at face value and I was shown the door, which was some sort of hand-carved archway imported from Spain. It wasn't until later that I heard about this man Luften."

"Ah, Luften," said Blake. A name he recognized. "Let me guess. You ran across Luften in a seedy bar in the Florida Keys. You poured out your troubles to him, and knowing that you had no cash available, he agreed to whack your ex-husband for a modest payment of vintage muskets and crystal ducks. It's what any average person with justice on their side would have done, and I don't see how any jury would see it differently."

"I first heard about Frederick Luften," said Loren, shooting her old schoolmate a glare, "from one of my few friends at Redding Enterprises. We bumped into each other at a bar—"

"In the Keys," filled in Blake.

"—in Hartford and she told me she had overheard Tom talking about this fixer Luften. She wasn't clear on the details, but apparently Tom had agreed to turn over a ton of cash to him with the understanding that he would hide it from the divorce settlement."

"A low trick," said Warren.

"And that's why I'm here. I don't know why Tom picked Uncle Chet and Aunt Deirdre's place for his corporate retreat; but whatever the reason it seemed the perfect place to confront him and ask him why he was doing this. I think I wanted to know about the orchestra more than anything. If he hadn't had me fired I never would have come after his money, and he wouldn't have had to hide it. The whole thing didn't make any sense, and that's what I would have told him. Only I never got the chance."

"And you were in the crate, because——"

"I told you, Warren, I was hiding. I was hiding because I had gone to the room to look for this. " She reached into her jeans and handed over a snarled booklet of paper. "I found it in Tom's shaving kit—it has a false bottom. I might as well give it to you now. You will learn about it soon enough. It's an insurance policy. The same friend who told me about Luften told me about it. I'm the sole beneficiary. I couldn't fathom why, after all he had done, Tom would have arranged to leave me any money, and that's one of the things I planned to ask him. After he was killed, I knew I had to find it."

"So you could collect?" asked Mahrute.

"So I could destroy it. It gives me a perfect motive for killing him. I knew as soon as the state police took over, they'd find it, false bottom or not. They're no dummies. No offense, Uncle Ernie. Uncle Chet and Aunt Deirdre also figured the cops would rip the inn apart looking for clues, and among the clues they would find would be me. My only chance was to get rid of this policy first."

Blake didn't know about the rest of the room, but he was satisfied. It all seemed to fit. "Good. And now we have the policy and if someone will simply hand me a lighter, that will be that. Will you do the honors, Sheriff, or shall I? We can use the wood stove."

Sheriff Ballard wasn't looking too keen on a campfire. "Loren, you should have told me you were here. Deirdre should have told me. We're family for goodness sakes! I might have helped you somehow."

"Like you're going to help me now, Uncle Ernie?"

"What is everybody talking about?" asked Blake. Everything was going along so well and now he was confused. "Sheriff, will you or will you not hand me a lighter?"

"I'm sorry," said Ballard. "I'll take that if you please. Evidence."

Blake was aghast. "What are you doing? It's not like she killed the guy or something." He turned and whispered, "You didn't, did you? Cough once for yes, twice for no."

Loren must not have had a tickle because she didn't make a sound. The officer apologized again, and together they headed for the door.

If Blake was aghast before, he was aghast-er now. "You're actually going to arrest your only niece?"

"I have six nieces, sir, and four nephews."

"Well, maybe they will all fit in the paddy wagon together. You can't do this, Ballard!"

"Don't make this any harder than it has to be, sir."

Blake liked making things hard. "But— But—" He looked to Mahrute, but for once the bodyguard had no encouraging words to offer. He went to the second string. "Warren—"

Warren stepped forward. Something had been on the tip of his mind since this conversation started. "What about Luften?" he said, snagging it at last.

Sheriff Ballard shook his head sadly—the same way he would have shaken it at a hunting buddy who had taken a potshot at one of the duck decoys. "There is no Luften," he replied.

"But— But— Dammit, that's what you said," Warren remarked, staring at Loren.

She shook her head. Must be a family trait, he concluded.

"Uncle Ernie's right. I had a private dick look into it a while ago and there is no Luften. He doesn't exist. Whoever helped Tom hide his money was a ghost, and the reason I called you that night was I thought you might be able to put a face with the ectoplasm. But you didn't know any more about him than I did. Tom had only hired you recently."

"But—"

"And then the shooting started, and I realized whoever was behind the Luften persona wasn't going to take my snooping lying down. He's smarter than that."

"You think the shooter was gunning for you?" asked Warren, shocked at this unseemly paranoia on her part.

"It doesn't matter now," she said, and went off to spend the night in Ballard's lockup. She hoped her cousin, Deputy Roger, was up for a marathon session of Gin Rummy.

☙

Well after they had gone, Blake remained motionless, a pony-tailed statue. His life was passing before his eyes. Not the boring old pointless life of the last two decades—what he would have considered more of a bland life substitute—but the life preceding it, when he had known Loren Hamilton. What sort of life had he since? College, a job he detested, two failed engagements he never talked about, each lasting only slightly longer than her marriage.

The twenty minutes they had spent together in her Toyota Land Cruiser had packed more pleasure and comfort into his life than the last twenty years combined. And now she was leaving, and he was standing there doing nothing about it.

He stirred. He moved his legs, and shot from the room. It was no good. She was gone.

Warren and Mahrute drifted out into the hallway, the former chiding the latter for not doing something more constructive, like chopping the sheriff in the brainpan. He didn't know what good it was knowing how to chop things, if you let perfectly good brainpans like the sheriff's go by unchopped.

"What do you think, Harvey?"

"Grr," said Harvard Blake, and punched a picture of a caribou.

"Harvey agrees with me. But what I want to know is why does everyone keep saying there is no Luften. It's really starting to annoy me."

Mahrute, though eternally respectful, pointed out that no one had ever actually met the man.

"If you don't call climbing into bed with someone and pointing a gun at their head meeting them then you must have a very rigid view of human contact, Mahrute. And what about Peterson? Peterson definitely met him. They must have talked in the lounge. And I saw him leave later, remember, but his face was in shadow."

Mahrute hated to be a constant drain on the deductive process, but detective work isn't all shootouts and femme fatales. "Mr. Peterson told the police that he never actually saw or met Mr. Luften, but was informed of his presence in the lounge by the innkeeper Deirdre. Deirdre does not technically remember the conversation, but in her own words, she tells lots of people lots of things and can't be expected to remember all of it."

"But someone must have seen him. Showed him to Redding's room, asked him where he was going with that bloody golf club, something. You sure you didn't see anything, Harvey?"

Blake was immersed in thought. Scenes from his life were playing before his eyes again but not the good parts with Loren. These were the annoying parts he had spent with Eliot Peterson the night of the murder.

"Peterson," he said, and went off to do something about it.

Warren didn't know what this was exactly, but he didn't like it. The way he had trudged off—past Trevor Green screwing in yet another lightbulb in the lobby; past Judith Carr yoo-hooing at him from afar; and onward and outward into the garden, having told the motivational speaker to "Stuff it, Judy,"—was not the Harvey they knew and loved. In Warren's opinion, he looked like a man about to spontaneously combust, or at least forget to type up Warren's recipes on index cards, as he had promised.

"Harvey seems upset about something, Mahrute."

"Indeed."

"He keeps muttering the name Peterson, like he wants to talk to him or kick him in the *cojones* or something. Perhaps one of us should go see what's eating him."

"I will see what I can do," said Mahrute.

He left Warren alone with his thoughts. Just Warren and the little bodyguard within.

The outer Warren stood watching the hotbed of treachery and deceit that was the lobby of the Berwald Island Inn. Trevor Green. Judy Carr. Some guy who had jumped in line at the breakfast buffet two days ago. All suspicious. All suspects. All to be avoided, said the outer Warren to himself, and the inner Warren agreed with him.

It was not long after this that the little bodyguard within went out for a six pack, or wherever it is that figurative bodyguards go, and Warren slowly became aware of a treacherous and deceitful presence standing beside him.

Vanessa Skinner had emerged from her lair.

She had gone to her room to paint. She always painted when she felt frustrated, having once, after a particularly vexing "job" in Bolivia, completed an entire series of dandelion fields, numbering one through sixteen.

After listening to her associate Trevor Green's pitiful explanations of how he had let their patsy Harvard Blake get away, she might have easily tackled dandelions seventeen through one-hundred-and-ninety-five.

Vanessa had been very angry with her associate Trevor, but now that Loren had taken the rap, she was cooling down. Any distraction was a good distraction, as far as Vanessa was concerned.

Considerably bucked up, she had already begun painting a finch nest from memory and had done it cheerfully and without rancor.

"The sheriff," she said to Warren now, "he is allowing us to leave the town shortly?"

Warren shook from his meditations. He wasn't listening. "Huh? I'm not sure."

"This murder has tried on all our nerves, I think. But it draws to a close?"

"Peanut butter, I guess," he answered, still not listening.

Vanessa switched gears. "I was doing the canvases in my room. The watercolors. You would care to see them, maybe?"

Warren looked blank, still only vaguely aware of her presence and the seductive tone of her voice.

"You do not like the paintings, perhaps?" she asked.

"Paintings? Oh, paintings. Yeah, paintings are fine."

"You would see them, then?"

"I don't know. Can't I see them from here?"

"There is a great distance, no?"

Warren supposed it was a distance. He wouldn't have called it all that great. "Actually I was about to pick some basil."

"That is your therapy, the cooking?" She oozed closer. She placed a slender hand on his beefy forearm and squeezed. "You will have a drink with me this evening. You will find it very therapeutic too, I think. Shall we say midnight, my room?"

Warren did not say, but it didn't matter because Vanessa Skinner had already faded from the scene. She left behind Warren, a handful of milling guests and Trevor Green, dusting his hand free of the lightbulb he had just crushed in his palm.

Warren didn't really want to have a drink with Vanessa, but he supposed it couldn't hurt. He may have misjudged her. She was obviously a nice girl. Nice and wholesome. A painter.

He left shortly thereafter, giving a friendly nod to the handyman, and went out into the garden to look for Harvard Blake. He wondered if Harvey had managed to catch up with Peterson. And if he had caught up to him, had he kicked him?

Warren hoped he had. If anyone needed a good kick, it was that fink.

15 – Working Overtime

As it happens, Blake did not meet up with Eliot Peterson that afternoon and consequently had no venue for kicking him. He only wanted to talk to him anyway. Talk plainly and possibly with a view to kicking him at some point in the future, but for starters, just talk.

Even talking appeared to be denied him on this rotten island. After scouring the garden, banging on his room door, and inquiring after him to Deirdre, Blake began to sense that their little chat would have to wait. He returned to his own room to think.

There was a simple enough reason why he had failed to unearth Peterson. The executive assistant wasn't aware that there was a garden and therefore hadn't visited it; he hadn't seen the inside of his room since breakfast; and the innkeeper Deirdre, when pressed for his whereabouts, was under the impression that his name was Paul. So solved the mystery of the unattainable assistant.

But hours later, a new mystery regarding Eliot Peterson would now emerge, beginning with him stepping out from his room at ten of midnight and peering up and down the hall.

Proceeding cautiously, he crept out into the corridor and eased silently down the stairs. Reaching the landing, he glanced over his shoulder and trickled into the lobby.

During normal business hours, which twelve a.m. was anything but, the entrance to the Berwald Island Inn was a lot more lively.

But at this hour, or any hour after ten p.m., it slept in darkness. The fireplace, regularly ablaze, sat dormant; the piano lay silent; and the moose's head, a common spectacle to guests, failed to work its spell.

It was exactly as Peterson had hoped. No witnesses.

He came to a door, and with a quick look back at the darkened room, pushed it open.

Three-quarters of the way across the threshold it hit an impasse—this impasse responding "Gurburf!"—and Peterson leapt back into the shadows, his perfectly round glasses gleaming in the moonlight.

"Who's there?" he demanded.

Some seconds later, the door pushed out again, and a prominent forehead emerged. Below this forehead was another pair of specs, also gleaming.

Peterson sighed. "Oh, it's you, Blake."

Harvard Blake sniffed. He set a bowl on the ledge of the counter that ran between the dining room and kitchen and removed a handkerchief from the pocket of his robe—a burgundy garment with yellow paisleys.

"You made me spill my bisque," he said, dabbing at the silk.

Eliot Peterson was not an emotional man. Some would have even called him stoic. But these words moved him deeply.

"Did you say bisque?" he asked. He licked his lips.

Like all things Peterson, there was a perfectly reasonable explanation for his current resemblance to a hungry mongoose.

It began earlier that day, around three in the afternoon, about the hour when Blake had come to the assistant's door and knocked. Peterson had, in fact, passed that time in the detached business center. A detached man himself, he found the place soothing. After the shambles at the seminar in town, he had needed all the soothing he could get.

At precisely six o'clock, he had returned to his room, showered, shaved, and at half past the hour was standing outside this very dining room, waiting to be seated at his regular table.

He never got it. Famished yokels, many of whom had jeered at him as he was yanked from the Judy seminar that morning, had descended on the hotel in record numbers, having heard told of Warren's wondrous soup. As Deirdre would explain to him on her way through to the kitchen, there was no room left at the inn; not even for paying guests like you, Paul.

Peterson had taken it in stride. He had ordered a modest supper to be sent up to him, returned to his room and fell asleep on his bed, waiting for it. (One of his fellow guests, a Paul Nelson, had enjoyed the meal very much.)

So explained Peterson's midnight journey. Although he hated making himself conspicuous, and hated even more admitting that the idiot Kingsley's soup was the finest he had ever tasted, he had made his trek for a reason, and that reason was staring him in the face.

"Was it lobster bisque?" he asked.

"It had a sort of lobster air about it, I guess."

"Finished with sherry?" wondered Peterson. The bisque Kingsley had served for lunch yesterday had been finished with a tantalizing aged sherry. Was this bisque that bisque, he inquired.

"I have no idea," snapped the other man, about fed up with contributing flowery descriptions to Warren's concoctions. What did sherry matter, tantalizing or not so tantalizing? When you had lost a woman like Loren Hamilton, it was all just soup. "I didn't ask it."

"Do you recall if any remains?"

"I didn't notice. Kick me my dinner roll, would you? It's by your foot."

Peterson booted the item as requested, and Blake picked it up and dusted it off.

"Thanks."

Beyond the fact that they both wore glasses, worked at Redding Enterprises, and were allegedly members of the human race, Blake wouldn't have cared to acknowledge anything in common with the miniature assistant. They were complete opposites as far as he was concerned. But there was one other experience they currently shared. Blake had also gone without food that evening.

His fast had nothing to do with crowds, nor the fact that Deirdre's husband Chester thought his name was Stanford. He hadn't eaten because he had spent the entire evening calling in favors, trying to get Loren a good attorney.

After making his final call to a friend in England, he had decided that justice moved too slowly for him never to eat again, and had come here in search of sustenance.

And right out of the chute he had run into Item One from his agenda, the slinking slime Peterson.

The slinking slime attempted to move past. "If you'll excuse me, Blake."

"Where do you think you're going?"

Peterson backed up a pace. The other's tone, normally so deferential, had surprised him. His reply was courteous if not a touch sardonic. "The bisque awaits. Or, looking at it a different way, it doesn't await. It all depends if you spilled the last bowl."

"YOU spilled."

"As you say. The point is not so much who spilled it, but what remains unspilt. Phrasing it another way, on the other side of that door there is either bisque or there is not bisque, and with your permission, I will now iron out the mystery once and for all. I'm starving." He thought he had made a fairly compelling argument, especially for twelve a.m., but Blake didn't budge.

"I've been waiting to talk to you."

"Wait a little longer."

"I know what you've done, Peterson."

"At the moment I'm only concerned with what I haven't done. Eaten."

"Why did you tell the police that you never saw Luften?" asked Blake.

The question gave Peterson pause. For an instant, hunger took a backseat to discretion. "Because I never did."

"That's not what you told us. I was in the room with the boss, remember? You said Luften was waiting to see him. You said you had dumped him in an armchair in the lounge but you didn't know how long he would stay there. What do you have to say to that?"

"Figure of speech."

"Then you're saying that Deirdre told you he was in the armchair, inferred all on her own that he looked antsy and itching to talk, and yet forgot the whole conversation a few hours later."

"That is what I'm saying."

"You killed Redding, didn't you?"

It took a lot to make Eliot Peterson laugh. Indeed, not since the age of six when a circus performer had mimed a steamboat towing a barge across the harbor had he even cracked a smile. (Peterson liked steamboats.) Blake might not have had the mime's comic timing, but Peterson still let out a short, rapid chuckle.

"You're saying I killed Mr. Redding?"

"That is what I'm saying."

"Have you forgotten that I have an alibi? You."

"Exactly what I wanted to talk about, Peterson. Why me? Why did you suction onto me that night?"

"Merely lost in the pleasure of your company, I suppose."

"Impossible. I'm not that interesting. And are you forgetting that I wasn't even there the whole time?"

Peterson removed his glasses and gave them a long, thoughtful polish. "I believe there are others who can vouch for my whereabouts after you left."

"Yeah." Blake had questioned the yuck-a-pucks from marketing. The alibi stood. "But that's my point. Why the yuck-a-pucks, Peterson?"

"Pardon?"

"Why go to all the trouble to surround yourself with humanity that night? You don't like humanity any more than I do. Your motives conceal a more sinister purpose."

"An amusing theory," said the assistant, still polishing. "The most compelling part is how well it proves that I never left the business center. Whatever my motives, you cannot deny that I hadn't the opportunity to leave the building for a minute, much less to murder our boss."

"You could have hired Luften to kill him."

"As I think the police have amply proven, Frederick Luften does not exist. Someone gave the name to the front desk the night of the murder, no doubt to clear the room of you and myself. I didn't give the name. Our good innkeeper might not remember talking to me about Luften arriving, but surely she would have sufficient faculties not to relay a message to me after I had only moments before relayed it to her."

"You could have had an accomplice."

Peterson smiled. He didn't laugh, he had already met his quota on laughing that evening, but he definitely grinned—unpleasantly, in Blake's opinion. "Or I could have nothing to do with the murder. Unless you have proof to the contrary?"

"I'm working on it."

"Take all the time you need. And while you're at it, perhaps you will consider this. I had no motive whatsoever for killing Mr. Redding."

"Well then, you must be the murderer," Blake remarked, happy to find that even smug little executive assistants can slip in their speech. "The person with no motive is always the murderer in these things," he said. With these stirring words, he removed his own glasses, and began polishing them right back at his suspect.

Peterson continued to grin. Or so Blake figured. He couldn't quite make it out, but through a kind of blur he fancied he discerned a sneer of contempt.

"This wouldn't have anything to do with the girl, now would it, Blake? Mr. Redding's ex-wife. Am I mistaken that she was arrested this afternoon?"

"You're not mistaken."

"And now you are spouting these unformed accusations against me? It's sad, really. You're trying to get her freed?"

"I've made some calls."

"And gone to the sheriff with your harebrained ideas too, no doubt? Pleaded for her release?"

"There was a fair amount of pleading, yes."

"And what did the officer say?"

"Not to waste police time."

"Good advice. You must care for this woman a great deal."

"I do, and you would do well to leave her out of it."

"You would do well to leave yourself out of it, Blake, for her sake."

For several moments following this exchange, neither spoke. They just stood there, two strong men polishing their eyeglasses at one another. Blake had several more unformed accusations to offer, but these would have to wait. Right as he was preparing to spout them, the kitchen door behind him opened and he toppled backwards into the darkness.

A muumuu-enwrapped body stepped over him. Deirdre had taken the stage. "What in blazes is going on out here?"

Blake was once more back among the vertical. He cinched up his bathrobe and dusted himself off. The gesture reminded him of his dinner roll, which had tumbled off into the great unknown, never to be kicked again.

"Deirdre," he replied, replacing his glasses on his face.

"It's no good saying Deirdre. What do you think you're doing sneaking around down here, Harvey?"

"Sorry, Deirdre."

"It's no good saying sorry. It's almost one in the morning. I— Hey, who's that lurking?" she asked suddenly, noticing Peterson with a shudder. "Who's that pipsqueak?"

Eliot Peterson stepped forward. He didn't like to lurk if he could help it.

He didn't like people referring to him as a pipsqueak either, but he kept this to himself.

"It is I, madam. Peterson. Mr. Blake and I were partaking in some leftover soup."

Blake nodded, supporting this.

"That's all well and good, but you two young scalawags ought to be in bed."

"Yes, ma'am," said the two young scalawags.

"Meanwhile, I'm looking for my husband. You seen him?"

Oddly enough, Peterson had. "I bumped into him earlier. He had with him a contract from whom he termed the herb people, and wanted to know if I would look it over for him. I think he thought I was a lawyer."

"Aren't ya?"

"No, madam."

"Well, you have no business looking like one if you're not. And what do you mean, contract? The Bensons are supplying us with herbs and produce, what's the contract for?"

Peterson explained that, from what he saw, it appeared that the contract detailed some kind of business venture her husband was contemplating making with Benson Farms.

"What sort of business deal! They grow herbs. There are no business deals to be had there. I swear, that man could overcomplicate boiling water. And where's he hiding anyhow? What's taking him so long with this so-called contract?"

Peterson had no information on this. He turned the floor back over to Blake.

"You know how these business contracts are," the latter remarked.

Deirdre said she didn't.

"Well, if you did, you would," he replied. "If it's anything like the contracts I've seen in my time, it's probably led to a lot of back and forth discussions. You know the sort of thing I mean. Lots of Person A not liking Person B's provision in Paragraph C, this followed by Person B saying now that A mentions it he never particularly cared for Subsection E, to which Person A tells Person B where to get off, and B says something nasty about A's ancestry, if A has an ancestry, and, well, you get the gist."

Deirdre turned to Peterson. "Is that how it works?"

"Not precisely."

The innkeeper snorted. "I don't know what you two are talking about. Maybe you're both drunk. I don't care. All I know is unless Chester turns out to be the second corpse found bludgeoned with an identical nine iron, he better start talking to you, Paul, about filing divorce proceedings."

"My name is Eliot, madam, and as I have already informed you, I am not a lawyer."

"Don't overcomplicate things. You and my husband! Could overcomplicate air. If I've told that man once, I've told him a thousand times," she began, and in what probably struck Blake and Peterson as a very welcome coincidence, the man appeared, perhaps to hear it for the one thousand and first time.

"Chester, what do you think you're doing?"

Her husband stood frozen. In his right hand was the infamous contract; in his left a posy full of fennel, picked fresh from his office greenhouse. He had come to really like the smell.

"Hiya, Deirdre."

"Don't hiya me. What's all this about a contract?"

"Contract? Oh, you heard about that? It truly is a most exceptional offer. I— Oh hey, Mr. Blake, the very man I was looking for."

"Don't change the subject by looking for Harvard. Harvard isn't the point. What are you doing mucking about with contracts and business? And with the Bensons no less! You know their family owns restaurant chains, don't you? They will eat you for lunch, Chester."

"It's funny you should say that because—"

"You're not a business type. You have no head for it. Remember the wheelbarrow supply job, and the gutter cleaning franchise? Fiascos. When it comes to business you're like that old song 'Misty.' As helpless as a chicken up a tree."

"I believe that's 'kitten,' dear."

"Kitten? Why would it be kitten? A kitten would have no trouble in a tree. A chicken, though— Throw one of them up a tree—"

"I think I'll be going to bed," said Blake, inching away.

Deirdre continued uninterrupted, "And what's even more unfathomable, you're playing businessman when you should be hiring attorneys for our niece. Someone like What's-his-name here—Benjamin. She was arrested today, if you didn't notice."

"I know she was arrested, Deirdre, and if we're going to hire someone to defend her, we'll need money. Ernie already pledged some funds of his own—"

"Don't talk to me about Ernie," said Deirdre. "I have no brother. Other than Larry, John, Albert and Rufus, that is."

"—and we can make up the rest if this deal goes through. It truly is the most remarkable—"

The words trickled off.

"Did anyone else hear a gunshot?" he asked.

Approximately fifteen minutes before Chester heard his gunshot, and around ten before Peterson and Blake had gone to the mat over murder and lobster bisque, Trevor Green was in his cabin, the modest abode afforded him as handyman.

He was in the corner of the room, rifling the closet.

His rifling had begun two minutes previous and he continued to rifle for another four, vocalizing his frustrations in louder and louder bursts. Finally the expletives ceased, and he emerged, huffing wearily.

All over him, from rounded chin to pudgy ankle, he bore the unmistakable dust and cobwebs of one who has rummaged long and rummaged hard. In his right hand he held the fruit of his labor: a 9mm Glock, hidden in the crawlspace shortly after his arrival a week ago. He secured this under his arm, closed the closet door, took one last petulant swing at the cobwebs, and went out onto the grounds.

The night was brisk like all Berwald Island nights, and he moved rapidly to his destination.

From the garden path he proceeded to a dark corner of the inn. From the dark corner, he went to his trusty ladder. And from the ladder he climbed up onto a balcony.

He had arrived.

He began by peering into the room on the other side of the window. For roughly ten seconds (call it twelve), he surveyed the suite—so unlike his own quarters that he gave it twice the scrutiny he had intended—and then, reeling himself in again, slid back against the balcony wall.

It was official. He couldn't have been more conspicuous if he tried. He had used the ladder for a reason, to avoid meeting anyone in the hall and thus avoid drawing any unwelcome attention to himself. But if his stupid shaved head waggling in the window hadn't drawn any attention, he didn't know what would.

Fortunately, as far as he could tell, the occupants hadn't noticed him. This was partly because Vanessa Skinner, the room's primary resident, was expecting him. Even if she had caught a glimpse of something in the window resembling an over zealous greengrocer offering her a coconut, it would have caused her no concern. She always played it cool. The other occupant was her reluctant guest, Warren Kingsley, who rarely noticed things regardless.

Their liaison had begun promptly at midnight, though it is debatable whether the word "liaison" really said it at all. (Unless one meant to describe a binding agent used in sauces, made up primarily of egg yolks. That sort of liaison they certainly could have been having).

Warren had brought the drinks: a bottle of bourbon he had swiped from the hotel bar. He was not entirely devoid of etiquette. He seldom drank himself—in his own words, alcohol made him kinda fuzzy-minded—but his hostess was welcome to all the stuff she cared to guzzle. He was a gentleman.

Drinker or not, he wasn't in much of a festive mood this evening. Anyone unfamiliar with his mental prowess would have said he was deep in thought. That may be overstating it, but he was clearly rolling things around in his mind—as close as he came to deep thought.

He was thinking about Loren Hamilton, wondering how she was doing, hoping she was getting enough exercise in the "yard." That

is, if women prisoners get yards. Maybe they gave them patios, Warren mused. Patios on which they could lie out in the sun, wearing
their prison issued bikinis.   And a volleyball court, where disputes
among the inmates could be settled, springing and bouncing in the
sand, until one of their prison issued bikinis gets snagged in the scuffle and—

Warren was very concerned about Loren Hamilton.

He was also concerned about Frederick Luften. He was wondering how a man who didn't exist could be taking shots at him all
weekend?

Finally, he was concerned about soup. This, more than anything,
occupied his thoughts. As with any artistic genius, he was feeling his
previous achievements were all well and good but he required something new to challenge him. He needed something exciting and fresh
and utterly amazing.

He needed a new lunch special.

His inability to think of anything exciting or fresh or even mildly
amazing accounted for his distraction, making him even more oblivious than usual to Vanessa's cozy behavior.

He ignored her sensual depictions of her life as a painter, over-
looked her pouty lips and softly seductive eyes, and gave her no reaction whatsoever when she ran her fingers up and down the back of
his neck in order to simulate the stroke of the brush.   Had Loren
Hamilton tickled the back of his neck, perhaps to demonstrate a piz-
zicato on her violin, he would have curled up beneath her fingers, a
mass of brawn and male hormones. But Loren was different. An
unspoiled beauty, a goddess of the earth. Vanessa just made him uncomfortable; her finger tricks reminding him of the time a boyhood
friend had slipped a bumblebee down his shirt back: okay for the
moment, but always mindful of the sting.

At a quarter after midnight, she desisted with the fingers and
took to running her palm up and down her bare thigh. At eighteen
minutes after, something seemed to penetrate the bedrock and Warren turned to her with wide eyes.

"Gotta a pen?" he asked.

"The pen—?" she began.

"I left my notepad in my room and wanted to jot down some
ideas for tomorrow's lunch. Could I have one of your stationery
pads too?"

"You can have anything you want in this room," she said, undoing a button on her blouse.

"Really? Doesn't Deirdre mind if you take stuff?"

"I am meaning—"

Warren said oh. Like bath towels and stuff. He always liked to snatch a few of those himself.

His abrupt departure from the sofa caused her to slump over on the cushion. She sat up, rubbing her shoulder broodingly.

"Something wrong?" asked Warren, scouring her desk for pen and paper.

"I am a little sore in this spot."

If Warren had any powers of observation, he would have realized that the spot she was rubbing was the same one Mahrute had chopped the evening of the brawl in the alley. The exact spot.

"It is the kink," she said. "It needs the careful massaging this kink."

Warren knew all about kinks. He still had that one in his back from carrying the Napoleon, and sometimes felt like he might be developing one in his triceps as well.

Massaging didn't help.

"You could always— Oh cool, one of those duck pens!" He began listing out his recipe.

Vanessa poured them each a bourbon. She scooted up to Warren on the sofa, the stud muffin back and scribbling away. She blew in his ear.

Warren looked at her and frowned. "This is never going to work."

"You do not find me attractive?"

"We're out of shallots," he said, and crumpled up the page. He would have to start again.

Out on the balcony, Trevor couldn't make out what was going on inside, but what he could see he didn't like. It looked to him like Warren was drawing her some kind of erotic illustration. Exactly the sort of thing a depraved character like him would do.

The handyman spy didn't know how much more of this he could take. He examined his Glock. Just wait, he whispered to it, just wait.

Somewhere down in the shrubbery, someone sneezed.

Inside, Vanessa wasn't sure how much more she could take either. She reached for her tumbler and raised the glass to her lips. She began to cough uncontrollably.

"Uck," she said.

Warren frowned at her. "Problem?"

She waved her hands and made a sound like a sensuous motorboat. "I have swallowed a ga-nat," she managed to say.

Warren looked confused. More confused than usual. "Swallowed a what?"

"Ga-nat," said Vanessa, "I have swallowed the ga-nat."

Warren understood. "I think you mean 'nat.' "

"What is not?"

"Not 'not'—gnat. It's pronounced 'nat.' "

"What is not? Uck! What is not pronounced?" she wanted to know.

"Huh?"

"What is not 'not'?" she asked.

"It's nat nice to swallow ga-nats," said Warren Kingsley.

Vanessa's coughing fit would not subside. The motorboat had become a more resonate steamboat-sound, the likes of which only Eliot Peterson could have enjoyed hearing.

Warren sighed. "Drink some water, why don't you."

Vanessa waggled her arms and sent the pitcher sailing off the coffee table. "Water, please." She pointed toward the bathroom.

Warren sighed again. He got up, retrieved the empty water pitcher and went to the sink. As soon as he had gone, Vanessa slipped a capsule into his glass.

Warren stood in the bathroom, staring.

The sinks at the Berwald Island Inn were all of a dual faucet design, one for hot and one for cold, and they never ceased to make Warren's brow twitch. He didn't care for them. You either got scalding hot or icy cold, never anything in between. There was no moderation about these sinks.

Of course, if you merely wanted to fill up a pitcher for a coughing woman, separate faucets weren't really a problem, but Warren still objected to them.

It was the principle.

Suddenly he froze, and not because he had splashed himself with the cold tap. He had had a breakthrough. A soup breakthrough!

"I got it!" he exclaimed, springing back into the sitting room without the pitcher or any water. Not counting the few droplets on his trousers. "What is the only thing wrong with soup?" he asked her.

"The soup?"

"Soup! Soup is delicious and good for you and it looks great in a bowl, but it has one significant drawback. It has to be served hot. Unless it's a gazpacho or something, and then it has to be served chilled. It's always about hot or cold with soup. I'm going to invent a soup that doesn't have this weakness. A soup that still tastes good even when it gets cold. Sort of like roast beef or really good pizza. A soup that warms you up in the winter and refreshes you in the summer. The king of all soups, a soup for the ages, a soup that knows no temperature!"

"Soup?" asked Vanessa.

"Soup," agreed Warren. He sighed contentedly. "I gotta go think this through. Can't hang around here all night."

Vanessa made one last desperate overture. "The drink? You have not drunk the drink."

"I'm not much of a drinker," Warren reminded her.

"It is for you to celebrate, no? The celebration of the soup?"

Warren paused. He could always drink to soup.

He lifted his goblet and said here's to ya. He paused, a couple of fluid ounces creeping over the rim toward his mouth.

He lowered it again. "Do you hear gunfire?" he asked.

Downstairs, Chester, Deirdre, Blake and Peterson had definitely heard it.

The sound of guns going off affects different people differently. Some gasp and whirl about, as though someone has kicked them in the seat of the pants. Others raise an eyebrow and say "Jeepers." Peterson belonged to the eyebrow school of thought. He frowned. He looked about himself with a cool head, and deduced. He didn't actually say "Jeepers," such strong language not suggesting itself in a woman's presence, but the word fairly played about his delicate features.

Chester and Deirdre, more excitable, gaped and spun about recklessly, jerking like a pair of window shudders in a stiff breeze.

Harvard Blake outdid them all. Neither a cool head nor a spinner-gaper, he showed his astonishment by standing completely still. While he stood, what remained of his lobster bisque drained out of the bowl he was holding and hit the tile with a splat.

Once these exhibitions had come to a close, the quartet hurried off in search of the gunplay.

They met many interesting people along the way. First on the journey was Judith Carr, standing outside her room in a long, pale nightgown. It suited her long, pale body.

She was curious about the sound too, but not curious enough to ask the man who had told her to stuff it earlier. Snubbing Harvard Blake with relish, she got her information from Chester, and soon joined the herd migrating up the corridor.

After Judy came Warren, still making notes. Behind him was Vanessa, beautiful yet sullen.

And then there was Mahrute, dressed in his typical three-piece and ready for action. One wondered when, if ever, the man slept.

Following Mahrute were a few of the Redding marketing yuck-a-pucks; then two women in curlers, then the man who had eaten Peterson's dinner; and finally, for dramatic tension, Loren Hamilton, back in her room and wearing sweats and a Beethoven T-shirt.

For this the herd had to pause. Several of the participants spilled into each other as those in the lead applied the brakes.

"Was that a gunshot?" she asked them.

The Berwald Island Seekers had no patience for irrelevant questions.

"Loren?" asked Harvard Blake and Warren Kingsley.

"Loren honey?" said Deirdre and Chester.

"Ms. Hamilton?" offered Mahrute. "You are not in custody?"

"Uncle Ernie let me go for lack of evidence. He said the state police will be here tomorrow and will likely have questions of their own, but till then I'm 'free.' So was that a shot I heard or what?"

The Seekers were satisfied. They answered that it was a shot, yes, a gunshot, coming from outside; and onward they went, out into the garden to seek it. Half of them were dressed in skivvies and nightgowns, but they didn't care.   They were searching for clues, dammit.

Mahrute found the first of these.

Beneath a balcony, next to an overturned ladder, lay a pistol.   A Glock, still in its holster.   He picked it up and sniffed the barrel.   "It hasn't been fired."

"But how can that be?" asked someone from the crowd.

"That's a neat trick," agreed another—and then from somewhere in the distance, there came a muffled gasp.   It was the kind of muffled gasp a person might make when struck in the back of the head by a small piece of brick.

"Get him off me!" cried a voice weakly.

The crowd backtracked.   Off the garden path, on the other side of a row of pine trees, they discovered Trevor Green flailing about in the moonlight.   He was sitting on his employer Chester, thumping the latter's head against the turf.

"Got him!   Got him!" he yelled.   Then seeing that he hadn't got him, he said, "Oh sorry, man."

He looked around at the spectators, and smiled sheepishly. "Thought he was the shooter," he explained.   He didn't bother to mention that he had spotted this shooter from Vanessa's balcony and in his haste to bound from the ladder, had tackled the wrong man. He didn't feel any of that was relevant.

He also didn't feel it was relevant to climb off poor Chester right away.   The innkeeper didn't seem to mind.   He was too busy groaning.

Behind them, Warren stood admiring Trevor's technique.   He stepped over to Loren Hamilton (too drained and befuddled to demand her uncle's release) and said, "See."

The sitting-on-perp maneuver, done to perfection.

16 – CUSTOMER SATISFACTION

Sheriff Ernest Ballard reached for the coffee pot and poured out two piping mugs for Warren and Mahrute. It was the following morning and they were in his office downtown.

The bodyguards were glad to have the last couple days behind them. Ballard was glad he wouldn't have to arrest his niece again.

"This man Trevor Green," he said, retrieving the cream and sugar from Roger (the deputy always tended to bogart the condiments). "He's a piece of work, all right."

Ever since bounding onto Chester the previous night, the substitute handyman had come under a good deal of scrutiny from the police. And so had his bonafides.

His behavior pretty much guaranteed an investigation. A shy, reserved handyman, who keeps to himself and never has a harsh word to say, one might easily ignore. But take that same employee and let him pounce on people and start trying to press their heads into the earth like a squirrel hoarding an acorn, and his cover, as Vanessa Skinner had termed it, will likely go *pa-fut*.

The authorities looked into things, and it turned out that Trevor's talents went beyond attending to the occasional wall sconce.

Ballard read off the highlights, "Barely made it into the FBI out of college, never excelled in any department, probably would have been drummed out eventually. Went rogue as a junior agent and was last known to be working with various crime families, helping them to track down snitches in the witness protection program. Piece of work."

Mahrute took this all in with a solemn nod. "And you believe Trevor Green murdered Thomas Redding?" he asked.

"Him or someone working closely with him. It all fits. Redding's business dealings touched all walks of life, including the criminal. It wouldn't be too much to imagine that he rubbed some individual the wrong way and they sent in Trevor to take care of it. We'll know for certain when we arrest him."

"He is not here?"

"Not at the moment. Shortly after jumping on my brother-in-law last night and breaking his arm, Green made a bolt. The state police are looking for him now, which I couldn't be happier about. Keeps them out of my hair."

Mahrute shared the sheriff's satisfaction, with certain reservations. "And the man Mr. Green replaced at the inn?"

"Hal Foster? Oh, Hal's okay—even if he is French. We think Trevor came along a week ago, looking for a way to get near Thomas Redding. Hal's injury gave Trevor the perfect opportunity into the inn. It was just good timing. We don't think he actually injured Hal or anything. Trevor isn't known to be violent—other than last night. And perhaps the murder. But other than that he's pretty soft. Normally he works with others who do the actual whacking."

"And the identities of these other parties?"

"No idea. When we find Trevor we'll probably find them. The state police is working on that too, and they always do their best, God bless 'em." Ballard sipped his coffee.

"Does the file mention the last job Mr. Green was working on before he went rogue from the bureau?"

"It does. Trevor was pretty low on the rungs, back office stuff, that sort of thing, but the stoolie they were due to relocate was hot stuff. Major Mob rat. I have a blurb on him here somewhere. Arthur Waterloo, I think his name was. Know him?"

"It doesn't ring a bell."

"I might have the name wrong. Give me a sec and I'll find the fax. Roger! Quit stuffing your face full of danish and help me find that file."

The mention of food, such as it was, shook Warren Kingsley from his trance.

The preliminary efforts on his special hot-cold soup were coming along nicely, and he was looking forward to returning to his kitchen and sampling version two. He also needed to see Eliot Peterson. Peterson still controlled the accounts at Redding Enterprises, and it was possible, with the murder all but solved, that the fink might agree to cut a check for Warren's services. Save everyone a lot of paperwork later.

With these two tasks in mind, Warren said his farewells and left to walk back to the inn.

Sheriff Ballard, meanwhile, had found his fax.

"Here it is. Let me see now. Oh, that's right. It wasn't Waterloo." He handed Mahrute the page, apologizing in advance for the jelly stain from Roger's danish.

Back at the inn, Harvard Blake circled the staircase, looking for Loren Hamilton. He probably should have sought out Eliot Peterson first and apologized for calling him a murderer, but he didn't feel like seeking out Eliot Peterson and apologizing. He felt like talking with Loren. He found her standing in Vanessa Skinner's old spot by the lobby window, gazing out at the landscape.

"Hi there!"

Loren favored him with a smile. It was a winning smile, but the sort of win that had come late in the sixteenth inning and cost each team four relief pitchers.

"Hi, Harvard."

"I've been looking everywhere for you. Is it true you're free?"

"Looks that way. The handyman Trevor is the man to beat for the moment."

"That's great! I can't believe you didn't tell me you were back last night."

"I went looking for you but they told me you were making business calls in your room. Tom was that way too. Even on the honeymoon. Must be something in the air with that firm."

Blake frowned. He disliked the comparison to her ex-husband, and he disliked even more the notion that his all-nighter had been in service of corporate greed. "Actually, Loren, I was calling for— I— Hold on a second, okay."

His phone *would* ring at this moment, and keep on ringing in that annoying chirp it had. It was like nursing an infant. "Sorry, just need to—"

"Make calls," she said. Tom used to answer calls in the middle of conversations too.

"Hello, yes, yes! Who? Oh right, the towing company. Yes, that's right. Right. Well, I want you to tow it—what do you think I want you to do with it? No, I know. I know it has no tires, that's why I want you to tow it. How's that? Well, of course you can't tow it with a chain—it has no tires. Right. No, I understand the physics behind it, I just don't understand why you're calling me. You're going to need a flatbed—flatbed. Well, what DO you call them on the island? I— Hold on." He pressed the phone to his shirt, gently shushing it. "Sorry, Loren, I—"

Loren wasn't there. Unknown to Blake, her uncle Chet had stepped out from his office, arm in a sling, asking for her to please help him unwrap his bran muffin. She didn't think Blake would even notice.

And yet he did notice. He noticed like the dickens. Back to the phone: "Look, I'll be right there. Forget the chain. Remove it from your mind. What? It's a sort of truck with a bed— Never mind. Touch nothing and I'll be right there." He hung up.

He went to the desk and called a cab. While he waited, he thought about Loren and wondered where she had gotten off to this time. He hated to admit it, but he was getting annoyed. Here he had gone to all this trouble coming to a realization about her and what she meant to him, and there she was treating him like goofy old Harvard, childhood screwup. He didn't understand women.

As if to illustrate this point, Judith Carr now appeared at his side. She needed to turn in her room key.

"Mr. Blake," she said coolly.

Blake looked at his watch. If the rest of the work force on the island was any indication, he would have a good forty minutes before his cab arrived. He could give Judy ten of these. He had something he wanted to get off his chest.

Down the hall, past the ice machine, Warren Kingsley hoped Peterson had something he would be wanting to get off his chest too. A nice, fat check.

He strolled to the door, and without knocking ambled in and sat down.

Although the maid service at the Berwald Island Inn was rare, Peterson's room sparkled. Eliot Peterson kept it that way. Even the papers he reviewed found their way into elegantly sorted stacks on his desk. It was into the midst of these elegantly sorted stacks that Warren, oblivious to the organization, put his feet up and opened a fruit juice.

Peterson fixed him in a cold, school-principal stare. "I would ask you not to put your shoes on our company reports, Kingsley."

Warren nodded and removed the offending clodhoppers, kicking Stack A into Stack B and dashing Stack C onto the floor.

Peterson attended to B. "Is there something I can do for you?"

"About my fee——"

"What about it?"

"I wouldn't mind it. If you got it."

"I have already posted a check to your agency."

"Oh good."

"Minus the expected deductions, of course."

"Deductions?"

"Mr. Redding is dead. Surely, you don't expect your full fee?"

Warren rather had, in fact. He should have known that the little dweeb wouldn't see it properly.

The little dweeb continued to glare. "Is there something else?"

"Not especially."

Silence followed. In the interim, Peterson returned to his work and Warren lay back watching the ceiling fan. "So do you think this Trevor guy did it?"

"I couldn't say."

"Me neither. Quite a night, though, huh?"

"Yes." At this moment in the dynamic exchange of ideas, Peterson looked up again, and this time not to glare at Warren. "Did you hear that?"

"Hear what?"

"Sounded like a noise. In the bathroom."

Warren frowned. "Must be the wind. Hey, do you know if this Trevor drives a brownish, blackish, sort of green sedan?"

Peterson wasn't listening. "There it is again. The noise. We should investigate."

"Never investigate noises," said Warren. "Killers like to make noises to draw people out. I can't tell you how many clients I've lost by them investigating little noises."

"When I said 'we' I meant you, Kingsley."

"You say you already mailed my check?"

"Yes?"

"I'm good," said the bodyguard, leaning back.

Peterson slammed down his pen. "How can you not hear that!"

This time Warren did hear something, shards of glass breaking and the distinctive sound of a gruff voice growling obscenities.

Seconds later, the bathroom door flung open, and a man staggered into the room. He wore a ruffled suit and carried a Colt .38 caliber revolver.

Peterson spun in his chair, quite put out by the visitor's unorthodox entrance. Warren, somewhat more put out, fell on the floor. Crawling as fast as his hands and knees would carry him, he popped up over by the bed.

For a few seconds, he scrunched there silently, gaping as he used to gape in school when the career counselor would ask him what he expected to do with a 2.1 grade point average. It was obvious that the man with the gun had introduced some highly perplexing concept with which Warren was now grappling.

"You!" he gurgled. "You're dead!"

The man, who had a different opinion, said "Ha!"

"What's going on here?" demanded Peterson.

"It's my ex-client!" Warren blurted out. "My dead ex-client, Andrew Hastings, the Mob informant, back from the grave!"

17 – EMPLOYEE BENEFITS

Harvard Blake's cab had arrived in twenty-five minutes, a new best, and Blake, having availed himself of its services, had spent another twenty-five arguing with the tow truck driver in the parking lot outside Nick Foster's antique shop. The driver, apparently not a certified towing professional, seemed unable to grasp the concept behind the Jag job. He was a traditionalist. His truck had a chain, and with this chain you hoicked and rolled a vehicle away, provided that it had the wheels to allow for this hoicking and rolling.

"Now look," said Blake, "it's very simple. You get a truck with a platform—"

"Excuse me there," interjected a third party.

Nick Foster, emerging from his shop, had come bearing gifts for Blake: two porcelain frogs, each two feet in length. "We forgot to give you these earlier. All part of the Redding order. Hold on, there is more in the shop." He returned two minutes later holding a giant bronze lily pad. For the garden. "Goodbye."

"Hold it right there!" shouted Blake.

"Hey?"

"I'm onto you, antique man." Blake scowled. Lugging a Napoleonic sword around Berwald Island the previous day had sharpened his consumer savvy, and he unsheathed this savvy on the shop owner now. "Redding didn't buy a damn bit of this and you know it. Even he had better taste than porcelain frogs. You figure with him dead you can go on padding the bill, knowing his estate will foot the charge. What do you have to say to that, junkman?"

Nick Foster had to pause and spit, that's what he had to say to that. "I have an invoice."

"Written out in crayon, no doubt. It may interest you to know that the state police are crawling all over the island. That's the real police, not your hunting lodge buddy Ernie Ballard. I'm sure they'd be happy to refer this matter to the fraud division, if I ask them."

Nick Foster spat again, but with conciliation in the gesture. "We don't need any of that. We'll just forget the whole thing, then."

"We'll try."

"Perhaps these items were not on the Redding order, after all."

"Perhaps not."

"We'll just forget the whole thing," said Nick. He looked like he might spit a third time, then appeared to reconsider. "You won't be telling the customer, then? Foster Antiques depends on her reputation."

"Considering that your customer is dead," said Blake, "I don't think I'll bother, no."

"Not Redding. I mean the other guy."

"I have no idea what you're talking about, my aged antique-meister."

"You know. The other fellow, the one who actually picked out everything."

"What fellow is this?"

"I cannot remember his name."

"You astound me. Someone on this island not remembering a name?"

"I have it written down. Hold on." Another pause. "And it is the Elk's Club me and Ernie belong at," said Nick Foster, "not the lodge."

With Nick gone, Blake had intended to resume his dialog with "Tow Truck Ted." Upon returning to the Jaguar, however, he discovered that "Ted" had left to get a snack or a towing license or something.

In his place was Bodyguarding Borodin. He looked agitated.

He wasn't exactly trembling under the pressure, but he had taken two deep breaths since his arrival, tantamount to hysterics for him. "I have come from the sheriff's office."

"No kidding."

"It was Andrew Hastings, sir."

"What was? Who's Andrew Hastings?"

"One of Mr. Kingsley's ex-clients."

"A dead one, you mean?"

"Normally, yes, I would mean that. There was a so-called accident at the time, but I don't think Mr. Hastings perished in it. I think Trevor Green tracked him here—it would be too much of a coincidence if he hadn't. I believe Mr. Kingsley might be in danger."

Blake didn't see how precisely, but was willing to string along with the theory. "I'll call for another cab. Probably be here in a couple weeks."

Mahrute nodded. He also apologized for his agitation. It was only that he had never lost a client before, and he did not intend to lose one today, even if that client always lost his.

His sang-froid was returning. He squinted across at the well-combed figure before him. "Excuse me, Mr. Blake, but have you misplaced your ponytail?"

Instinctively, Blake reached for the back of his head. He smiled. "Oh yeah. Judith Carr lopped it off."

"Vindictive."

"No, I asked her to do it."

Mahrute did not understand. Perhaps his composure had not yet returned.

"I'm sorry, I'm not explaining it properly. See, I had gone to Judy to apologize. I had spoken to her rather harshly and it wasn't right. She's a human being. An annoying human being, but a human nonetheless. She forgave me, and we got to talking, and it turns out she had once been a hairdresser. Apparently that's where she learned the gift of gab. I told her it was funny she should bring up hair because I had been thinking of changing my look. That's when she offered to help me out as a way of showing that there were no hard feelings between us. I think she did a pretty good job."

"Yes."

"She said it brought back all kinds of pleasant memories for her. She loved the work, and sometimes felt she was crazy to have ever left it."

"So this kind gesture on your part has pointed her along a happier path?"

"Not at all. She's going to go on consulting. She plans to meet with the world's hair trimming franchises and offer her services. Tell the executives how to discover the corporate hairstylist within, and explain how they can sheer away the locks of economic inefficiency."

"Pity."

"It is, yes. But she's happy and I can always let my hair grow out again. Say, do you think we should walk? The cab company said ten minutes, but that probably translates to two hours."

Mahrute had another thought, but before he could voice it Nick Foster rejoined the gathering.

"There, told you I had an invoice," he said. He handed this to Blake with triumph.

Blake studied the page. "And you say this guy picked out all the items? Mr. Redding never came into the shop at all?"

"Never once. The other one chose it all."

"Even the statue of Napoleon?"

"Especially the statue."

Mahrute looked over Blake's shoulder at the name scrawled on the sheet. "Peterson?"

"Eliot Peterson," repeated Nick Foster. "Picky little man. And the fuss he raised, when it was all his instructions to begin with."

"Fuss?" asked Blake. "Instructions?"

"When we brought the goods to the banquet. He seemed completely taken aback. But he was the one who had asked us to come to the business center. Specifically! We couldn't figure what he was playing at."

Blake's eyes lit up. He knew what Peterson was playing at. He still couldn't figure how Andrew Hastings entered into it, but he knew one thing for sure: unless they did something, Mr. Redding's real murderer was about to get off scot-free.

"Come on, Mahrute, we'll borrow the tow truck."

"My thoughts exactly," said the bodyguard.

Warren Kingsley sat on the end of the bed, rumpling Eliot Peterson's finely tucked covers. He looked across at the gunman and shook his head.

It was funny. It was only a few days ago that he had been telling Mahrute about poor Andrew Hastings, the stoolie whose car had careened off a cliff into the cold ocean depths below. Who'd have thought that he would come bobbing back into the picture now?

"I was sure you were dead."

"You just assumed I was!"

"Well yeah. I mean, you drove your car off a cliff. What was I supposed to think? So I guess you survived the fall?"

"I jumped out before the car went off the cliff."

"Nice. So that's why they never found a body in the water. So what's new?"

Hastings eyed the bodyguard angrily. "What's new? What's new! I'm going to blow your brains out, that's what's new!"

Warren appeared puzzled, if not somewhat hurt. "Blow my brains, Andy? Why?" He began to put things together. "Wait, it was you creeping into my room the other night?"

"Yes!"

"And in town? The sedan—"

"Yes!"

"Huh. Would you call your car blue or more of a racing green?"

Hastings waggled the gun at him, not inclined to talk paint chips.

Warren's brains, meanwhile, not yet blown, continued to gather speed. "Hold on! You don't think *I* cut your brake lines, do you?"

"Of course not. That would have required a basic level of intelligence."

"Right... So why the menace?"

"Because you're an incompetent bastard, that's why!"

Warren nodded. It was a compelling argument, but he still didn't follow.

"You almost got me killed! I hired you to protect me!"

"Oh that. That really wasn't my fault, Andy."

"The hell it wasn't! Where were you when my car careened down the mountain road? Where were you when I dragged myself to safety, half-dead and pursued by killers?"

Warren threw his mind back. It was a while ago. "I know I had a dental appointment that day—"

"I have been hiding out ever since. Laying low."

"Lying."

Hasting goggled homicidally, and Warren clarified, " 'Lying' low, Andy. The past participle—"

"Shut up! Do you know what I've been doing all this time, Kingsley?"

"Not really. Something fun?"

"Thinking."

"Good man. I often enjoy a spot of thinking myself."

"Thinking about gunning you down."

Warren sighed. His ex-client truly did have a one track mind. No wonder the Mob had opted to do away with his services. He looked over at Peterson, the twerp soaking this in through a pair of sparkling specs. Warren would have preferred a more sympathetic companion, but he took some satisfaction in knowing that the shooting would make a mess of the assistant's room.

"And don't think your broker is going to rescue you this time either," said Hastings.

Warren blinked. "Broker? Oh, you must mean my bodyguard Mahrute. He's very good, by the way. If you're still in the market, I'd recommend him."

He paused, struggling for some fascinating topic to keep the conversation going. As long as Hastings was talking he couldn't be shooting, and that arrangement appealed to Warren. He wasn't exactly worried about his safety, or worried about anything, really. In moments of distress his brain had the admirable trait of shutting down completely. It left just enough power in the system for idle discourse and standing upright, and other than that it was boarded up tight until the storm passed over. In the mettle-testing field of personal security, this often came in handy, though not always for his clients.

"Not that it matters, Andy, but how'd you get in here? You're not a guest at the hotel, are you?"

"I came in through the bathroom window."

"Isn't that a Beatles song?"

"Stop wasting breath, Kingsley!"

Warren agreed to try. "Something else just occurred to me, though. If you were the one who threatened me in bed, and you were also the one shooting at us, you must have been in town awhile. You didn't kill Redding, did you?"

Hastings let his gun arm drop to his side. "Of course not. Why would I kill Redding?"

"I don't know. Just thought I'd ask."

"Well, don't."

"Right. Just a passing thought."

"Well, keep them to yourself. You made me forget what I was going to say."

"Sorry. Something about crawling half-dead to safety?"

"No."

"Blowing my brains out?"

Hastings brightened. "Yeah, that's it."

"Now listen, about this revenge stuff. I'm sure it seemed like a good idea at the time. Kept you going while you passed your sad existence on the lam, subsiding on nuts and berries in the forest—"

"I lived in a Buddhist Monastery in Canada. They mostly fed me wheatgrass soup."

"We'll have to compare recipes sometime," said Warren. "But the point is, Andy, revenge won't do you any good. Surely the monks taught you that."

"After I told them about you, they let me use the gooseberry vineyard for target practice."

Warren said ah. Pretty forward thinking monks. "Look, I know you, Andy. You can't kill me. No matter what has passed between us, you're still my client, a client who had no problem crying in my presence when we watched the end of *Rocky I* together. Besides, if you truly wanted to kill me, you would have done it the night of Redding's murder. In my bed. But you couldn't pull the trigger."

"You kicked me in the groin!"

"Did I? In your *cojones*? Sorry, Andy—reflex."

"I couldn't shoot you after that because I was in too much pain and I could hear people moving in the next room. You also squawked like a train whistle."

"I don't remember squawking."

"Maybe this will refresh your memory," said Hastings, cocking the hammer.

Warren held up a hand. The nighttime janitor of his brain had flicked on a light in the back of his mind, and he felt compelled to attend to it. "Just one last thing, Andy, before you shoot. If you didn't kill Redding, maybe you know who did. I have a pool going with the deputy. He says Trevor Green acted alone, but I think he had an accomplice. Any thoughts?"

Andrew Hastings lowered his gun again. He glared. "Green! The fed who sold me out."

"Oh, that's right, you know each other."

"We know each other," said Hastings. "But he didn't kill Redding. That was the twerp," he remarked, jerking the Colt offhandedly toward Peterson.

Warren looked at Eliot Peterson. Sitting silently through all this, he had been waiting for Hastings to get on with it so he could get back to work. "Me?"

"Peterson?" Warren concurred. "Peterson, the twerp?"

"The very twerp."

Peterson looked amused. "I don't know what you're talking about."

"I saw the whole thing," said Hastings.

As befit his role as an informant, he had a wealth of information on this and many other topics in the criminal milieu.

"I had been hiding in the business center, waiting to off Kingsley. It was nice because hardly anyone ever came in there. The night of the banquet, though, plenty of people came, so I hid in one of the spare rooms they're remodeling in the back. Around eight, your boss Thomas Redding arrived. From what I could see from under a tarp, he looked like he was waiting for someone. At eight-twenty, someone came, but from the frown on Redding's face it wasn't who he expected. It was you, Peterson. I think you were talking with someone out in the hall. You stepped inside, carrying this little rolled rug. You set this down, raised a finger to your lips as if you were trying to keep Redding from blowing the gaff, and then as cool as you please you picked up a golf club and bashed the old guy in the head with it. It was not at all what I expected."

Peterson was speechless. So was Warren.

"Anyway, that's how I saw it," said Hastings, feeling that they could take it or leave it as they liked.

"You saw it correctly," said Borodin Mahrute, appearing in the doorway.

"Indeed," said Harvard Blake, poking his head in from the corridor.

18 – Employee Incentive

On a lark, Blake had armed himself with the Napoleonic sword from his room. He had intended to hand this into the Redding collection days ago, but was glad to have it available now. You never knew when the perps might decide to give you trouble. (Although, if Blake had known that one of these perps was going to have a gun, he might have reevaluated this thinking.)

Warren was delighted to see them. "Well done, Mahrute! I was just telling Andy here that you always arrive in the nick of time."

"No, you weren't," contradicted Hastings. He was a dour, sallow-faced man, and he had no patience for embellishment. "You never said that at all."

"I said he was very good as a bodyguard, and that implies that he has excellent timing."

"How do you figure? If you're a good bodyguard you should just be there, not stumble in half-an-hour late. That's the sort of thing you would do, Kingsley, except you wouldn't even bother to stumble in."

Warren shook his head. "I don't know why you won't let me have this, Andy. It doesn't matter. I'm just happy you guys are here. Even you, Harvey. Hey, what happened to your ponytail?"

At this point, Hastings broke up the discourse by banging on Eliot Peterson's dressing table. In the process, he upset a small bottle of aftershave and a pair of eyebrow tweezers. (Into the presence of the latter it is probably best not to delve.)

"Enough with the ponytail!" cried Hastings. He glared at Mahrute. The other still looked like a stockbroker to him; he didn't care what Warren said. "You witness the murder too?"

"I did not, sir. But I believe I know how it was done."

Warren held up another hand to their better armed visitor. "Don't shoot me yet, Andy, I want to hear this. Okay, Mahrute, go ahead. You say you know how Peterson did it?"

"Yes, Mr. Kingsley."

"Cool. What I want to know is how he killed him in the business center but somehow arranged for us to discover the body in a bedroom on the other side of the inn."

"Oh, that was no sweat," said Blake, doing loops with his sword. "That was you."

"What was me, Harvey?"

"You were it. You helped moved the body, my good man."

"I did?" asked Warren, also wondering why Blake was sounding British all of a sudden. He supposed the spirit of the thing had gotten to him, but he wished he would knock it off.

"Not literally, of course," Blake admitted. "Let's just say you helped with the illusion."

Warren continued to look blank.

"Perhaps I can take it from here," offered Mahrute. Blake nodded amiably. "The statue was Mr. Peterson's smokescreen, a diversion. Anyone who saw Mr. Kingsley and himself shifting Mr. Redding's belongings would only remember Mr. Kingsley struggling with the statue. It took quite an effort moving it."

"You bet it did!" said Warren.

"A chance witness to your activities would hardly notice at all the roll of carpet slung over Mr. Peterson's shoulder. The body was in the rug."

"Golly," said Warren.

"About that," Blake interrupted. "I know you explained everything on the ride over, but that point still bugs me. I saw the rug at the banquet and it was tiny. Miniscule. You're not suggesting that Peterson stuffed Redding's body into that?"

"Not at all. The tiny rug you saw delivered was a diversion."

"Another diversion?"

"Indeed. Mr. Peterson wanted it documented that a statue and a rug had been delivered. After that, he had no use for the actual rug."

"Now let me see if I got this straight," asked Warren. "Peterson lured Redding to the business center, telling him that Luften wanted to meet him there in secret. Redding went, waiting in one of the spare rooms, so no one from the firm would see him and ask him why he was slinking around talking to shady characters. Then Peterson, on the pretense of stowing away some of Redding's antiques, stepped into this room and without pausing for breath, bashed Redding in the head with an antique golf club he had left there earlier for that purpose. Okay, I think we're all happy with that. But then he rolled up the body in which carpet now? Carpets and diversions would appear to abound in your narrative, Mahrute, and I'm having trouble keeping track of them all."

Mahrute was happy to explain: "Mr. Peterson rolled him up in a carpet from the business center. As you have probably noticed, all the area rugs in the hotel are of a single pattern. I think if you examine the contents of Mr. Redding's room, you will find that he has two of the inn's rugs. One on the floor, which Mr. Redding was killed on and transported in; and one rolled up by Mr. Peterson and placed among Mr. Redding's many belongings. Anyone seeing it would mistake it for another of his purchases from the antique shop in town."

"Makes a difference from swiping bath towels, I suppose," muttered Warren.

Mahrute shifted around to face the accused. "Your plan was to divide and conquer. Mr. Blake had seen the small rug but would not be present while you carried the body across the hotel in the large one. Mr. Kingsley would be present for the carrying but had not seen the smaller rug arrive. As long as they did not get together on the matter, you had accomplished your goals. You had a witness to say that a rug arrived, and a witness who saw you in the process of carrying a rug back to Mr. Redding's room."

"But wait a minute!" spoke up Andrew Hastings, attending an itch on his ear with the muzzle of his revolver. "Are you seriously asking us to believe that this little twerp carried a body hundreds of yards across the hotel?"

"Mr. Redding was not a large man. He was thin and very frail."

"Even still. If he had been a little ol' grandmother I still don't see it."

"He's got a point," said Warren.

"Indeed," added Blake.

"Perhaps you would care to explain." Mahrute directed another respectful nod towards their suspect. "Perhaps not. Mr. Peterson is too modest to boast about his past, but years ago, in his youth, he won quite a few tournaments in the junior weight division of the Canadian Strong Man Competition. I looked him up on Wikipedia."

"Little Ellie Peterson?"

"He is quite fit. I first suspected this when I had to adjust the weight on the Nautilus machine he had used in the fitness room. It was set to an impressively high level. I personally had to move the pin up to a much lower weight setting."

"Amazing," said Warren. "Okay, last question. If this was all accomplished without an accomplice—a knowing accomplice—who did I see leaving Redding's room the night of the murder? Who's Luften? Who feels like fielding that one? — Ellie?"

Eliot Peterson did not immediately answer. These unwanted visitors had proven even more annoying than he had originally thought them. There was no point in perpetuating this façade now. Another minute's consideration, and he remarked blandly, "You saw Mr. Redding."

"Redding?"

"I had suggested he conceal his identity, should he meet up with anyone from the firm along the way. The hat and coat were the best he could come up with."

"Then I was right—he never intended to receive Luften in his room?"

"No. Long before the night of the banquet Mr. Redding had agreed to meet with Mr. Luften in the spare room in the business center. I had said that Luften wanted a neutral area in which to discuss their terms, and Mr. Redding had no real problem acceding to the request. Then again, he was under the impression that you would be there as well, Kingsley. If you recall, I was the one who told you Mr. Redding would not require your services the night of the murder."

"Like it would have made a difference either way," scoffed Hastings.

"Then there really was no Luften?" asked Warren.

"Of course not. I fabricated him out of thin air. I came up with the idea during Mr. Redding's divorce. I made Mr. Redding believe that he stood to lose a fortune in the settlement. Ms. Hamilton's behavior, unfortunately, did not support this—she was far too willing to let the matter lie. But once I had her dismissed from the orchestra, she came along to my way of thinking."

"You had her fired?" said Blake.

"Yes—although the request appeared to come from Mr. Redding himself. Loren Hamilton had to be properly motivated for the divorce, and this apparent vindictiveness on the part of her ex was the ideal spur. Once she had shown herself the properly scorned female, I went to Mr. Redding and told him that I had a friend named Luften who could hide some liquid assets for him in the Cayman Islands. Mr. Redding liked the suggestion and handed over the funds without a qualm. From there, all I had to do was wait and plan the murder. Once I had killed Mr. Redding, the police would put the blame on Luften, whom I would claim was Mr. Redding's associate and not mine. In order to set things in motion, I came to Mr. Redding a few weeks ago and told him that Luften was going to keep the money. I said he had started making demands of his own and was becoming menacing. Mr. Redding naturally wanted protection and I knew the perfect idiot."

"Hey," said Warren.

"There were a few obstacles along the way. There was more scrutiny over the Luften persona than I had anticipated. And, of course, the later shootings kept us here longer than I would have liked. But all in all, everything fit together nicely, I thought, and when Ms. Hamilton turned up—well, that was all gravy."

"Yeah, well, your gravy's gone cold," said Hastings. He might have spent time in the Mob, but he still took a dim view of all this chicanery. "You're a slippery little monkey."

Peterson focused an analytical stare at the informant.

"What?" the latter asked. He hated when people stared at him. Especially twerpy people with beady eyes.

"It's ironic, isn't it?"

"What?" Hastings repeated. "What's ironic?"

"Kingsley. We both want him dead. We both see him as an obstacle."

"That's not ironic," Warren asserted.

"These three men represent a very inconvenient loose end for me, Hastings. You could solve both our dilemmas here."

Hastings shivered. This slippery little monkey was really beginning to creep him out. "What?" he asked.

"You came here for a reason, Hastings. Do not hesitate."

The informant goggled at the gun. "Me? But I— I mean— What?"

"I have money. Half of it could be yours if you simply fire. Thrice."

"Don't listen to him," said Blake. "What does money matter?"

Peterson continued to push. "Think, Hastings. You could hide out pretty well with some ready cash. The Mob is probably close on your trail."

Hastings looked back and forth between Peterson and Warren.

Warren then Peterson. Mahrute then Peterson then Blake and back to Mahrute. The room began to spin.

"Shoot them!" Peterson commanded.

"But these guys didn't do anything."

"Irrelevant! What sort of Mafioso are you?"

Hastings gulped. "I was the boss's interior designer!"

"And no better man with crown molding," chimed in Warren.

Peterson frowned. He expected more from his criminal element.

He swiveled back around, shaking his head. "I see. If you are resolved to be difficult, there is nothing more I can say." He smiled softly. "Now if you will excuse me, something has been bothering me here for the last ten minutes." He pulled open a nearby drawer and reached inside.

A wave of determination swept over Andrew Hastings.

He might not have the capacity to gun down Warren Kingsley and friends in cold blood, but he wasn't about to let this executive pimple pull a weapon on him. Especially a pimple with superhuman strength. Jumping at Peterson's sudden movement, he plugged the guy without hesitation.

Peterson keeled over, gripping an object from the desk.

Hastings retrieved it. "What the hell is this?"

"Looks like a coaster," said Blake.

"For Kingsley's bottle," Peterson gasped. "It was making... nasty ring... on papers..."

Hastings nodded. "Sorry, guy."

He might have tacked on more substance to this apology, but at this instant the door flung open, and Sheriff Ballard shouted, "Everyone hold it right there!" Better late than never.

Hastings leapt back. The officer repeated his command, but the nimble-footed informant had already scooted back through the bathroom and out the window.

Ballard pursued. A moment later he returned, holstering his gun.

"He got away. I got a call to make." He paused at the door. "What's that?" he asked, indicating the lump on the floor.

"Peterson," said Warren.

"He dead?"

"Nah, he's one of the Canadian Strong Men. He'll be fine."

Peterson made a groan, and Ballard nodded and left.

19 – EXCESS CONTRIBUTION

There seemed to be very little to say after this.

This was not unusual. Whenever a deranged interior decorator/Mob informant (bent on revenge against an incompetent soup-making bodyguard) has gunned down a small ex-champion Strong Man, it is only natural that the participants in the room will experience a certain lull in the conversation. It is completely normal.

Harvard Blake said something along the lines of "Well, that was fun," and Warren muttered something about getting ready to make his spring before the shooting started. But other than that, not much.

Mahrute excused himself shortly therefore. He had a loose end to tie up. Actually two loose ends.

As he descended the back staircase, pondering these loose ends, he caught a glimpse of a furtive blur fleeing through a side exit.

Picking up his stride, he followed this blur out onto the grounds and halted it with a loud (though dignified), "You there!"

A thickset boy of about eight, curly-haired and freckled, twirled around in mid-scamper. He glared at his elder offensively. "I wasn't doin' nuthin'!"

Mahrute found that hard to believe. "You're one of the infamous Jenkins kids, are you not?"

"Maybe."

"Your siblings' exploits are well known in these parts, even to a stranger like myself. I would assume you're the youngest?"

"Maybe."

Mahrute could see that small talk wasn't the Jenkins forte. Pranks and auto theft, yes. Small talk, no. "Have you been here all morning?"

"I wasn't doin' nuthin'," said the boy. (Unless you counted overflowing the toilets in the first floor restrooms somethin', which the youngest Jenkins did not.)

"I'm curious if you saw a man crawling out one of the windows?"

"Nah."

"Think hard. He was in a suit, gray-haired and very frazzled."

"Nah."

"There is a reward in it for you."

"I did see a guy," said the boy promptly. "But he wasn't in a suit."

"Who was it?"

"Who knows? Some guy. He was in one of them plaid lumberjack shirts and his hair wasn't gray. There wasn't hardly any hair there at all."

"Are you speaking of Trevor Green, the inn's estranged handyman?"

"Sure, why not."

"The police have been searching for him, you know?"

"Sure, why not."

"Where is it that you saw him?"

"He's right there in front of you," said the boy, pointing.

Mahrute followed his crooked little finger.

There, a few inches behind the chimney on the roof, a head poked up against the horizon. As the boy had astutely observed, it hardly had any hair on it at all.

Mahrute smiled at it. Loose End # 1, there for the tying. And all thanks to this junior juvenile delinquent.

The bodyguard beamed with gratitude. He was put in mind of the young man who had faithfully fetched the prize goose for Ebenezer Scrooge at the end of *A Christmas Carol*. Mahrute wasn't prepared to gush as Dickens' miser had done, but he still felt the youth had earned his modest reward.

"Thank you, son. You——"

But the youth had gone.

Whether he had suddenly considered the whole process a little too much like grassing, or some far, far better prank beckoned, Mahrute was unable to say. He didn't mind. It had saved him a few bucks.

Around the corner in the kitchen, Warren Kingsley scooped out a sample of his special super-soup from the pot, attempting to place the whole jarring morning behind him. He had said it many times before——clients have no class. And this was especially true of ex-clients who were supposed to be dead. Not civilized. That was the word for them. Or rather not for them.

He sipped. Not bad. Not bad at all, although it could still use ginger.

He was wondering if a sprig of cilantro might do the trick instead, when he noticed a glimmer of movement reflected in the pot lid in his hand. It was humanoid in shape but very wiggly, as pot lids tend to make things. Wiggly or not, this reflection interested him immensely.

Turning to receive his visitor (and possible taste-tester), he was surprised to find Vanessa Skinner staring at him. He was even more surprised when he realized that the long pointy object in her hand was a chef's knife. It was with this knife that she was now lunging toward him.

Up above them on the roof, Borodin Mahrute alighted from a ladder onto the stone ledge that ran around the length of the house.

The tiles were flat here instead of slanted, but Mahrute found little consolation in this. He was not fond of heights. He minced across to the chimney and tapped Trevor Green on the shoulder.

The faux handyman sprang up at the touch. He had been brooding and the unexpected tap had scared the bejeebers out of him.

"It's you!"

Mahrute agreed that it was, none other.

"I should have known it would be you. Vanessa always said you were the one to watch out for."

Mahrute appreciated the compliment from Loose End #2. "You will be happy to know," he said, "that the police no longer wish to question you in connection with the murder of Thomas Redding."

"Oh good."

"They merely wish to question you in connection with the plot to assassinate Andrew Hastings."

"Oh darn. You know about that?"

"We do."

Trevor thought they might. "But how do you know so much? I thought you were only here to mind the dolt Kingsley?"

"I have many duties beyond minding Mr. Kingsley," said Mahrute. "I was originally brought in by your witness protection to investigate the disappearance of Andrew Hastings. When Mr. Kingsley put in his call to our agency, requesting reinforcements, I volunteered for the task. I already knew that Mr. Hastings was in Berwald Island and might try to make contact."

"We figured that too. Kingsley was supposed to lead us right to him. As soon as we heard Kingsley was coming here for the corporate retreat, Vanessa booked a room and I took the job as handyman. We figured with Hasting's life still in danger his old bodyguard might know where to find him. Hastings might even try to seek him out."

"Mr. Kingsley was, indeed, the person he sought out, though not for the reasons you supposed."

"When Hastings never showed, Vanessa got the idea of drugging Kingsley and making him tell us where his client was hiding. She put something in his drink last night, but the dolt never drank it. It didn't matter, though, because at that very moment I saw Hastings sneaking around the grounds. Before I could react he shot at me! *At me!* Then everything went to hell, and I thought it better if I hid out till the heat cooled down."

Mahrute thanked him for the recap. "Perhaps you will step this way."

Trevor didn't shift. "Have you ever been in love, Mahrute?"

The bodyguard preferred not to share such details with a man whose head looked like an oversized nectarine. Not to mention the fact that the rooftop was beginning to do the shimmy around him. He wished to go. "Mr. Green—"

"I ask because that's why I did it. I didn't mean to sell everyone out. I fell in love."

"Very moving. On the subject of moving—"

"That's why I did it, Mahrute. Not for the money. For love. I first met Vanessa in Barbados on a misty summer's afternoon—"

"I really don't—"

"Anyway, that's why I did it," said Trevor. "And why I'm doing this now," he frowned, producing a derringer pistol from the recesses of his flannel. "It's Vanessa's," he explained. "She let me have it after I dropped my 9 milli last night."

Mahrute rolled his eyes. For an instant the roof ceased to twirl, and he was the older, more experienced man of the world talking to the young agent who had lost his way. "This is all rather pointless, Trevor. Hastings is long gone by now. Shooting me won't help you."

"It doesn't matter. Vanessa wants some time alone with Kingsley. If he doesn't tell her what she wants to know, she'll gut him like a two-hundred pound trout. Which reminds me, what does he put in his bouillabaisse? My grandma used to make bouillabaisse, but even hers didn't compare to his. He has the knack."

Mahrute was in no mood for talking soup. "As I have already indicated, Mr. Kingsley does not know anything. Neither of us does. Mr. Hastings did not confide in us."

"Not important. She'll gut him anyway. Help to salvage something from the wreck. When she goes back to our clients, she can say, Hey at least I got that bodyguard fella Warren out of the way for you."

Mahrute doubted that any criminal would welcome this news. Warren Kingsley was one of the criminal world's greatest assets.

The handyman was stroking his derringer again. "Two bullets," he remarked. "One for you, should you prove ornery, and one for

Warren, should Vanessa have any trouble finishing the job. It's not the way I wanted it, but I promised."

Mahrute was touched.

Down below, Warren sprang and jutted out of the way of Vanessa's blade. She didn't appear to be having any trouble finishing the job.

He answered her lunge with a grand pirouette, scattering herbs and spices and nearly tripping over a stalk of celery. Foiled by the maneuver, Vanessa recoiled to a short distance, wriggling her wrist ever so gently. She was very practiced with the blade.

Warren was shocked and disturbed. Was this the same woman who had tickled his neck the night before? It looked like her but she was different somehow. Little less made-up perhaps. Far less pouffy in the hair. And way more homicidal.

"Is that one of my chef knives?" he asked.

Vanessa didn't answer, and Warren changed the subject.

"This isn't because I forgot to look at your paintings last night, is it? Because we can go see them right now if you want. I won't even yawn."

"This has nothing to do with paintings!" exclaimed Vanessa. She advanced and pressed, meeting Warren's pot lid and pushing him off with a shapely thigh.

For a fleeting moment Warren caught her wrist, and in the exchange he had a realization. "It was you in the alley, wasn't it? You're the assassin?"

"Of course I am the assassin!" she shouted, and tried another moulinet against the frying pan in his right hand. "I have always been the assassin!"

"Ah. Then you're not a painter at all." And here he was feeling guilty for overlooking her canvases.

"Of course I am the painter!" she declared, swinging the knife with renewed energy. She hated it when her victims ignored her art. "I am the painter as well. I first learned the skill," she said, slashing this way then that, "as a sniper. The high up perches, they give me the overhead perspective which would later become my signature approach."

"Cool," said Warren, dodging that way then this. He always liked to hear about a fellow artist's approach. "But on the subject of your day job, you've been trying to kill me all week, haven't you? I thought it was only Hastings."

He was beginning to think that these folks should start a club or something. They could have their meetings at the Berwald Island Inn.

"It was originally not to kill, no," she said. "In the alleyway, I was only trying for the submission. Trevor was waiting behind the dumpster with the hypodermic. Once drugged you would tell us the whereabouts of the informant Hastings. It is he that I am here to kill."

"Cool."

A few more seconds of steamy knife-on-pot action, and Vanessa asked the obvious question: "Where is the informant Hastings?"

"No idea. He was here a minute ago," Warren remarked. "Did you say that Trevor's in on it with you?"

"He is the rogue agent. He does this for the love of me. I let him because the good help is so difficult to find these days."

Didn't Warren know it. "Then you weren't trying to kill me? The knife in the alley was only for show?"

"It is my weapon of choice since taking up the brush and the canvas. They are very similar, no?"

Warren supposed they were, if you painted bloody messes. "Still —and don't think I'm being critical—you really could have injured me. You were pretty wild that night."

"There are many ways to cut a man without killing him," said Vanessa, an expert in the field. "I would have only immobilized you."

"Gotcha. It was an immobilizing knife. And this one?"

"This is a stabbing knife," said Vanessa, demonstrating the principle.

She had worked him over into a corner, and no doubt would have proceeded to show him how much of a stabbing knife it was, had a sudden distraction not caused her to lose her focus.

Harvard Blake had entered the kitchen. He was whistling happily and twirling, appropriately enough, his Napoleonic sword.

"I have been meaning to tell you, old bud—" He halted midsyllable and stood blinking at the carnage and celery scattered at his feet. "Um, I can come back," he said.

Vanessa would hear none of it. She whipped across the kitchen toward him.

Unaccustomed to women showing him this kind of ready passion—and almost never with cutlery—Blake gasped, dropped the sword and jumped onto the counter beside the sink. He folded his knees against his chest and cringed for the slice.

Inches from her destination, Warren tackled her from behind. Blake watched with goggling eyes as the pair wrangled about on the tile below him, grappling for the knife. There was something vaguely sensual about the whole thing.

"Dammit, Harvey, do something!" yelled Warren, and Blake threw half a lemon at her. When this proved ineffective, he reached for the hose on the kitchen sink and sprayed.

He sprayed to no avail. Vanessa was on her feet again, looming over the prone bodyguard, her knife at the ready. Then she slipped on the wet tile and was off her feet.

Somewhere between the lemon and the spigot Blake had rediscovered his *cojones*. He bounded off the sink, scooped up his sword and was holding her at its tip now, as if no countertop had ever come between them.

"We make a pretty good team, Warren."

Warren scowled. He had hit his head on the tile and skinned his knee on the dishwasher. And he was wet. Very wet.

"Where's Trevor?" he asked Vanessa.

With the leader of their gang immobilized, he didn't relish the thought of a monkey wrench to the back of the skull, care of that deranged, lovesick handyman. It was the sort of thing Trevor would do. It also hadn't escaped Warren's notice that Mahrute was conspicuous by his absence. His bodyguard might be in danger.

"Where is he, you Norwegian psychopath?"

The assassin sneered. She slid across the checkered tile and leaned her willowy frame against the wall. "I am not Norwegian," she said, "and I tell you nothing."

"Tell me or I make sure everyone hears that you and the pinhead Trevor were lovers. Hot and steamy lovers. Couldn't keep your hands off each other."

"He's on the roof," she replied. Warren had found her weak spot.

On the roof, the pinhead Trevor was having trouble keeping Mahrute with him. The bodyguard had already traversed the distance from the chimney to the ladder and was preparing for the long, trying descent to earth (hopefully not more than one rung at a time).

"I said stop!" whined Trevor. Why didn't anyone ever listen to him? People were supposed to listen to people with guns.

At that height, he wasn't at his most sure-footed either, and couldn't quite match Mahrute's practiced mincing. "Stop or I will shoot you!"

Mahrute said he would expect nothing less.

"I don't want to shoot you, Mahrute, but I will."

"My client requires my services," said the bodyguard, reaching out for the ladder.

Oddly enough, no sooner had he secured the top rung than his client's head rose up from the void beneath, blinking up at him in the sunshine.

The sudden appearance of a head where no head ought to have been affected Trevor much as Eliot Peterson's grab for the coaster had affected Andrew Hastings.

He fired.

Warren spotted the flinch and from out of nowhere his long dormant bodyguarding instincts took over.

He whipped Mahrute to the side with a mighty shove, slightly ahead of the blast.

One thing hadn't occurred to him. With Mahrute out of the way, the projectile was now free to strike the next solid body in its path. Warren's solid body.

It hit his right shoulder. It was the first bullet he had ever taken for anybody, and for a moment he simply stood there, musing on it.

At first, he felt nothing. He was beginning to see what Mahrute had meant when he had spoken lightly of flesh wounds. It was rather flesh-wound-y, now that he thought about it.

Then the pain set in and Warren did not see it as a flesh wound any longer. He saw it as a major freaking agony.

He cried out "Son of a bitch!", and fell off the ladder.

His only desire now was to land on something soft. A ton of cotton balls would have been nice, but he would have settled for a shrub, provided it didn't have many pricklies.

The ladder had other ideas. As he tipped back into the brisk sea air, Warren's shirt cuff snagged the rounded post above the top rung, and he hung there, dangling.

Had he been wearing one of his Argentinian shirts the cuff would have easily given way. But Blake's designer brand was not so easy to displace. The cuff stood firm against the tug, refusing to budge, and Warren swayed this way then that, a well-dressed piñata.

By now Trevor had closed the gap between them. With about ten feet left to go, he raised the derringer to discharge the second bullet.

He squeezed, but not before a pinstriped blur flashed in front of him, absorbing the shot. Borodin Mahrute had returned to the fray, and taken one for the team.

"Dammit! Knock that off, you two," groused Trevor.

He was speaking to an empty space. The force of the blow had sent Mahrute over the edge of the roof. He had met up with Warren on the way, and together they had ridden the ladder all the way to the ground. One long, gut-wrenching arc, and they hit the grass in a clang of metal and muffled oaths.

Vanessa Skinner and Harvard Blake had heard the clang in the kitchen. Neither thought anything of it.

"So, have you been a heartless killer long?" he asked.

Vanessa said, "Well—"

Loren Hamilton ambled in across from them. "Warren, have you seen Har—"

She paused, taking in Harvard, the sword, and the slinky girl in the wet T-shirt.

"I can come back," she said.

Blake called after her. His movements were somewhat restricted, holding Vanessa in status quo, but that didn't curb his desire. "I want to talk to you."

Loren stepped over the pots and food stuffs and said, "Where'd your ponytail go, Harvard?"

Blake said never mind his ponytail.

"I won't if you won't. You want to talk to me?"

Blake did, but he had to arrange his mind first.

During the interval, Loren introduced herself to Vanessa, and the artist-assassin returned the courtesy.

The swordsman finally spoke up. "What's the opposite of love at first sight, Loren?"

"Hatred over time?"

"No. No, that's not it at all. I'm doing this all wrong."

"Speak from the heart," Vanessa encouraged him from the floor. She knew about these things.

Blake thanked her.

"Loren, I'm not going to feed you some line. I'm not going to say that you've always been the girl for me and that I have spent countless restless nights dreaming about you and me as a couple."

"Oh good. Girls hate that."

"Until recently, I never even thought of you as a girl at all."

"Thanks."

"What I mean is, we were friends. Good friends once. But I never saw you for what you were, Loren. What you have become. A wonderful, caring, beautiful woman, whom I would really like to get to know better. As a woman. You as a woman, I mean. I'll stay a man."

Loren seemed to think that that was probably the best arrangement. "What are you saying, Harvard? Are you looking for a new girlfriend or something?"

"I don't know what I'm saying. I just know when Ballard carted you off yesterday, something in me felt lost without you. And then you came back and it sprang to life."

"He's talking about his pee-pee," said Vanessa.

"I am not talking about my pee-pee!" Blake vociferated. "I don't know what I'm talking about. All I know is I sound like a complete sap saying it. But I don't care. I want you in my life, Loren. And I can help you. It tore me up inside hearing about your shattered dreams. I can help you with that. I'm good at it. If I can talk my way into Oxford University, then I can certainly talk you back in at the Bath Chamber Orchestra. Talent like yours shouldn't be wasted."

"Oxford University?"

"Yes?"

"Oxford University is not a quiet country college!"

"It's a college," argued Blake, "and it's in a country. But never mind that. Forget Oxford. I'm here for you, Loren. If you want me."

Loren climbed over Vanessa. She stroked Blake's arm, which, unless she was mistaken, was moist with lemon juice.

"I'd love your help, Harvard. I'd welcome it. But only if you really want to do it. I'm not a project. Tom saw me as one, and looked what happened."

"Someone conked him with a golfing stick," Vanessa reminded them.

"Our marriage was a flop. I don't want our relationship, wherever it is, to be a flop too."

Blake was in agreement. No flops for them. "Then we'll—I don't know—date?"

"For starters."

"Awesome."

It was during the subsequent embrace, somewhat encumbered by the sword, that Sheriff Ballard burst into the room. He was doing a lot of that today. His revolver was drawn and his eyes were wild and roving.

"What the hell is going on?" he asked.

Blake should have anticipated this reaction. These quaint New England towns have their traditions, and these traditions have to be upheld and respected.

"Sheriff, I have the honor to ask your permission to pursue your niece. In a romantic, romancing kind of way, I mean." He looked at Loren. "It sounded better in my head."

She thought it sounded fine. Finely fine.

Ballard could make no sense of it. He looked at his niece, then at Blake, and then shook his head in the manner of a wet Saint Bernard.

"What were those gunshots?"

"Oh those. I thought I heard a shot or two. Weren't they yours?"

"No!"

"Ah. Then I'm sorry to say I can't help you, Sheriff."

Ballard had gathered that. "Who's that?" he asked, gawking at the female on the floor.

"Vanessa Skinner," answered Blake.

"She's an assassin," said Loren.

Ballard nodded again, and went off in search of those gunshots.

Trevor Green sprinted across the grounds toward the downed bodyguards.

He had already reloaded the derringer with the refills Vanessa had given him earlier. (Somehow she had known that two shots wouldn't cover it.)

With his ladder lying in a heap on the lawn, he had been forced to find another way down from the roof. Fortunately he had one. Shortly after Warren and Mahrute's impromptu acrobatic act, he had dashed over to the drainpipe, skimmed from this to the trellis, and from the trellis he had tumbled down into the garden. Easy.

Neither Warren nor Mahrute had shifted much in the interim. Mahrute was unconscious, draped over to the side, gushing a dignified amount of blood. Warren was awake, but he was shot and wet and also gushing blood, and on top of everything else his ankle was entangled in the ladder rung. On the plus side, the kink in his back felt pretty good.

Trevor scrambled over to where they lay. He held up a hand a moment to catch his breath. This done, he pointed the gun, closed one eye to assist accuracy and—

Immediately staggered backwards. A .38 caliber slug had hit him in the right arm.

He fell over, resolved never to try and shoot anyone on behalf of a stupid girl again. It wasn't worth it, he realized, seconds before passing out.

From somewhere in the direction of the shot, another voice, older and gruffer, was also cursing the inequity of life.

Andrew Hastings, the man behind the gun, peered out from behind a pine tree, grumbling woefully. The shot that had struck Trevor, the last one in the chamber, had actually been aimed at Warren Kingsley.

Nothing was going right on this trip, Hastings said to himself, and fled the scene a step ahead of Sheriff Ernest Ballard and deputies.

20 – TIDY PROFIT

An hour later, the town doc had finished stitching up Warren and Mahrute in the garden. Eliot Peterson and Trevor Green required more extensive medical attention and had been taken into town under the supervision of deputy Roger, who was considering asking for a raise. Sheriff Ballard had arrested Vanessa Skinner, and everything was more or less back to normal at the Berwald Island Inn.

Sitting on one of its stone benches in the afternoon sun, Warren turned to Mahrute, sitting beside him.

"So that's what it feels like taking a bullet for someone," he said—although, technically speaking, he hadn't exactly taken the bullet. The bullet had taken him. "Is that how it always feels?"

Mahrute replied that it was more or less the routine, yes.

Warren nodded. "I don't like it," he remarked, and Mahrute conceded that it was not for everybody.

In the midst of this philosophizing Blake and Loren strolled over. They wanted to inquire after their friends' injuries. These niceties completed, Blake slapped his forehead. "Oh Warren, I almost forgot."

"Forgot about what, Harvey?"

"Forgot to tell you about the incredibly awesome offer. You know that place Benson Farms?"

"No."

"It's the place where we got the herbs from. Anyway, that little rascal Chester—you know, the innkeeper—he worked out this ridiculously amazing deal with them."

"What kind of ridiculously amazing deal?"

"I'm telling you. From what I understand, a few days ago he called them to complain about something, who knows what, and they got to talking soup—your soup—and these Benson people want to buy it."

"Lunch is served between noon and three."

"I don't mean a bowl. I mean the whole kit and caboodle. See, they own restaurants all over the world. You might have seen one of them in town: the Czech Around Café."

"Czech Around Café?"

"No doubt established when such plays on words were fresh and amusing. Anyhow, they own restaurants, but they're looking to get out of the business. They want to go into a whole new line selling dishes in the frozen food aisle."

Blake could see he wasn't winning over his audience with his motivational speech. Judith Carr might have managed it, but she was a professional and had presentation boards and slides and things. He wasn't coming across.

He decided to forgo the rest of the preamble and give them the gist with both barrels.

"They want to buy your recipes, Warren, and market them to supermarkets!"

"Oh yeah?"

"Yeah. It's the chance of a lifetime! The money is very, very good. Chet and Deirdre will get some, because it was their inn that made your soup famous. I'll get some, as your agent. And this money, added to the swag Loren is getting from Redding's insurance policy, will help us start a life together."

"Are you starting a life together, Harvey?"

"Didn't you know? Well, we are. And it will be a whole lot better than her life with Thomas Cranky-Pants Sr., I can tell you that."

"Oh, don't talk about Tom that way," said Loren, awaking from the rather lovely daydream she had been having. "Remember, all the stuff we thought he had done to me in the divorce, wasn't him at all. It was all Eliot Peterson. And the insurance policy—that was all

Tom, the Tom I married. He must have signed it over to me without Peterson's knowledge. That's probably why Tom hid it from him."

Blake declined to go into the thought processes of his late employer. But Loren's point was well taken. There is good in all of us. "Anyway, I think that covers everybody. Money for me and Loren, money for Chet and Dee-Dee—"

"What about me, Harvey?" asked Warren. "They're my recipes!"

"Oh sure, money for Warren too. Definitely. Well, what do you say?"

Warren didn't. He sat and massaged his wound. "I thought you had plenty of cash?"

Blake was shocked. Shocked and amazed. "I don't have two beans. My family has gobs, but I renounced my right to any of it when I refused to go along the chosen Blake path, starting at Harvard Business School. Why doesn't anyone ever hear that part?"

Loren gave his arm a sympathetic squeeze. "Sometimes people tune you out, honey. You do tend to talk a lot," she said, still sympathetic.

Blake supposed he did. He struck his serious face. "Listen, Warren, about this soup deal. We don't have to do it unless you absolutely agree. I'm here for you. I'm your guy."

"I don't want to do it, Harvey."

"I've already told them that we would. I mean, we can go back on it now, I suppose. But they've started spending money on promotion. There might be a breach of verbal contract. Raised voices. Haughty sighs. I don't think—"

"Yes, okay, whatever," said Warren.

"We can do it?"

"Okay, yes, whatever."

Blake rejoiced. "Good man. Wait here while I fetch the contract. Coming, honey?"

Loren said she was. But not before she paused and thanked Warren and Mahrute for all their help. Especially Warren. He was a wonderful man, she said, a strange and wonderful man.

Warren watched as she joined Blake on the veranda. His agent kissed her warmly and turned and waved back at them from the doorway. It was the thumbs up which followed the wave that really irked Warren.

"I liked him better with the ponytail."

"I'm sorry if this disrupts your plans," said Mahrute.

"Nah. I was thinking of getting out of soup anyway. Too cut-throat. I have actually been thinking of starting my own bodyguard agency."

"Indeed?"

"Makes sense, I think. I'm still suited to it, as long as I don't have to take another bullet for anyone." He stood up and stretched his good arm. "Guess it's time to pack."

Mahrute fell in step with him along the garden path.

"There is one soup-related thing I'd like to perfect some day," said Warren, as they walked toward the house. "My masterpiece. Something the gum-heads at Benson Foods will never get their claws on."

"It sounds fascinating."

"Oh, it is. But before I explain about it, a question. What is the one downside of soup?"

Mahrute considered this a moment and then answered, "I suppose that would be its temperature control. Soup must either be served hot or served chilled. Hot soup, therefore, gets cold, and chilled soups gets warm."

"Exactly!" Warren knew he could always rely on Mahrute. He led the way over the horizon with his bodyguard and friend.

Further Reading

I f you enjoyed *Double Cover*, don't forget to check out Warren and Mahrute's further adventures in *Five Star Detour*.

Books by Sherban Young

the Enescu Fleet series

Fleeting Memory
Fleeting Glance
Fleeting Note

the Warren Kingsley series

Five Star Detour
Double Cover

more books

Opportunity Slips
Dead Men Do Tell Tales

CPSIA information can be obtained at www.ICGtesting.com
Printed in the USA
BVOW08*0113101213

338636BV00001B/5/P